SIX O'CLOCK HOUSE

&

OTHER STRANGE TALES

BY

REBECCA CUTHBERT

Also By Rebecca Cuthbert

Non-Fiction

Creep This Way: How to Become a Horror Writer with 24 Tips to Get You Ghouling

Short Story Collections

Self-Made Monsters

Six O'clock House & Other Strange Tales

Poetry Collections

In Memory of Exoskeletons

Children's

Down in the Dark Deep Where the Puddlers Dwell

SIX O'CLOCK HOUSE
& OTHER STRANGE TALES

REBECCA CUTHBERT

Published by Watertower Hill Publishing
Joshua Daughrity - Publisher
www.watertowerhill.com

Copyright © 2024 by Rebecca Cuthbert. All rights reserved.
www.rebeccacuthbert.com

Cover and internal artwork by Susan Roddey
at The Snark Shop by Pheonix and Fae Creations.
Copyright © 2024 Watertower Hill Publishing. All rights reserved.

No part of this book may be reproduced in any form without prior written permission of the author and publisher—other than for "fair use" as brief quotations embodied in articles and reviews.

Author's Note
All character and names in this book are fictional and are not designed, patterned after, nor descriptive of any named person, living or deceased.
Any similarities to people, living or deceased is purely by coincidence.
Author and Publisher are not liable for any likeness described herein.

Library of Congress Control Number: 2024950366

Hardback ISBN: 978-1-965546-05-5
Paperback ISBN: 978-1-965546-06-2
eBook ASIN: B0DN4GRXQ2

Printed in the United States of America
10 9 8 7 6 5 4 3 2 1

This collection is dedicated to Joel, who makes me believe

again and again

that I can do anything.

It wouldn't make for sanity, would it, living with the devil.

-Daphne Du Maurier

PRAISE FOR SIX O'CLOCK HOUSE & OTHER STRANGE TALES

"A collection of intimate wounds sutured with strange delights, Cuthbert deals in haunting contradictions. Rarely have I been so grateful for heartache. A smile that cracks through a sob."

--Jamie Flanagan
Bram Stoker Award-winning writer and actor

"There's no doubt in my mind that Cuthbert is slugging it out with the modern greats. Few short story collections have thrilled and immersed me as completely as *Six O'Clock House & Other Strange Tales*. Usually, the thought of diving into another story right after finishing one feels daunting, but here, you can trust that the next will be just as excellent—if not better. Cuthbert masterfully channels the unique essence of each character, so whether you're reading about a naive waitress, a sex-crazed teenage boy, a city man thrust into country life, or a woman advocating for herself in an abusive situation, you're bound to fall in love. This collection isn't just a keeper—it's top-shelf material."

--Christopher O'Halloran
author of *Pushing Daisy*

"Welcome to a fantastic house of mirrors like no other. These characters are worn out and weary but still charged by the magic that lurks just beneath the surface of their lives. This is a dark magic. And Cuthbert serves it to us with both grit and grace."

--Sarah Gerkensmeyer
author of *What You Are Now Enjoying*

"Cuthbert skillfully takes ordinary characters and settings and adds touches of fears and fable, to create strange tales that are the perfect mix of eerie and unnerving. Oozing with unease and tension, this is a collection that is sure to get under your skin."

--Lyndsey Croal
author of *Limelight and Other Stories*

"With this collection, Rebecca Cuthbert infuses horror into the cracked lives of protagonists haunted by the past, their jobs, and sometimes even their own selves, proving that it doesn't have to be midnight for dread to creep down your spine–the stories in *Six O'Clock House & Other Strange Tales* will unsettle at any hour."

--TJ Price
author of *The Disappearance of Tom Nero*

"In Six O'Clock House and Other Strange Tales, Rebecca Cuthbert reaches deep down into the reader's gut, grabs hold of those secret fears, anxieties, and heartbreaks we all keep hidden, and rips them right out through the throat--a painful yet necessary experience--bringing the bloody yet beautiful horror of everyday life out into the light."

--Heather Daughrity
Best-selling author and editor of *Echoes of the Dead, Knock Knock, Tales My Grandmother Told Me*, and the "HoH Anthologies Series"

PUBLICATIONS AND AWARDS

"Joiner" - Finalist in the 2021 New Millennium Writings Award

"Bait & Switch" - Published by *50-Word Stories* in an earlier form

"A Bargain at Twice the Price" - Honorable Mention in the Onyx Publications Winter Contest - Published in *Etched Onyx Magazine* and read on the *Story Discovery Podcast* (2021)

"Punching In" - Finalist in the Crystal Lake Shallow Waters flash fiction contest, time theme (2023)

"Rest for the Wicked" - Published in *HAUS: Anthology of Haunted House Stories* by Culture Cult Press (2022)

"Thick on the Wet Cement" - Published in *The Future Fire*, then selected for its ten-year best-of anthology, *TFFX* (2015)

TABLE OF CONTENTS

Praise for Six O'Clock House & Other Strange Tales ix

Publications and Awards x

Foreword by Lindsay Merbaum xiii

Joiner 1

Tumbling After 19

Hey, Stranger 21

Infested 47

Lovesick 59

Bait & Switch 73

A Bargain at Twice the Price 75

Funeral Hats 91

Thick on the Wet Cement 95

Six O'Clock House 103

Danger: No Swimming, No Fishing 117

Inheritance 129

Punching In 145

Poor Billy 149

Rest for the Wicked 163

Damp in the Walls 167

Readers' Discussion Guide

About the Author

Additional Titles by Rebecca Cuthbert

Acknowledgments

FOREWORD BY LINDSAY MERBAUM

I first encountered Rebecca Cuthbert in 2022 when she enrolled in a virtual feminist horror class I was teaching. The conditions were just right and the group sparked kinship.

Recognizing this magical occurrence, Cuthbert helped turn that class into what we now call the Study Coven: a community of like-minded women writers exploring the strange and unusual.

Over the past few years, Cuthbert has recruited a whole host of study witches. She is a natural gardener; whatever she touches, grows.

I'm honored to call her a friend and co-conspirator.

You may believe, upon entering our author's latest collection, that you're in familiar territory: a small town bar; a crappy service job that could be worse; a situation-ship with a married guy who's a little *too* into you.

Now look again.

That loquacious server is happily chatting up a killer. This patient's therapy literally manifests her past selves. A stray donkey is munching on bananas, while the living replay the fates of the dead. And horror of horrors, there's a data entry time loop.

Cuthbert keeps revising our expectations of what horror is and can do. Case in point: the title story in *Six O'Clock House & Other Strange Tales* applies new meaning to the term "bed rot."

In this piece, a florist's assistant suffers from body shame and the loneliness of being rejected by the one she loves the most.

The shop is also home to an eerie greenhouse, tended by an unflappable older man. Could he be Death himself, the Lord of Decay?

In "Poor Billy," Drew's father warns him he better tidy up, or "Poor Billy" is going to come take all his toys. The threat is off-handed, a casually inflicted fright.

But then Drew's toys begin to disappear. It's not Drew's father–he's forgotten about the whole thing. Drew's little brother doesn't even pick up his own toys.

It must be Poor Billy; he's real. Drew takes some very grown-up steps to rectify the situation, until he comes face-to-face with his final challenge. How much is Drew willing to sacrifice? But more importantly, why should he, a child, have to make such impossible choices?

Why is Drew the only one looking out for himself and his younger brother?

When Poor Billy appears, the scene is at once chilling and gut wrenching. A manifestation of neglect and abuse, Billy looks like the beat up ghost of a murder victim. He is, in a way, Drew's doppelgänger, or perhaps the specter of the boy's father's own childhood.

You could read this story as confronting parentification, a type of abuse where children are forced into a parental role over their sibling(s). The potential for trauma and suffering is amplified by the father's disbelief: ironically, he doesn't think the specter he himself conjures is real. He rejects the reality he's created for his children.

Six O'Clock House & Other Strange Tales ends with another fraught domestic scenario: a classic haunted house tale, or so it seems. In "Damp in the Walls," a couple with a troubled relationship buys an old home, which they soon discover possesses many mysterious problems. Jen gets pregnant and begins having hallucinations–or are the visions and bad smells real? Her partner Kevin is oblivious. He's also abusive.

The cycle of violence peaks just as Jen enters her last trimester, when she's at her most vulnerable.

A deadly storm hits but Kevin refuses to evacuate. Reader, here you prepare yourself for Jen to die giving birth. For her to drown, or sacrifice herself to save her baby. Because this is what we know about women: abused characters get abused.

Final Girls are always a bra strap away from annihilation.

I won't tell you what happens to Jen. All I'll say is, it's not the ending you have been conditioned to expect. Water gives and takes. It also cleanses.

Under the skin of this story, and others, there's rage. A Medusa's-laugh kind of rage. Bitter, honest fury. The kind that turns women into complicated monsters, and archetypal monsters into prey.

Welcome, reader, to Cuthbert's domain.

Lindsay Merbaum is the founder of Pick Your Potions and the author of The Gold Persimmon *and* Vampires at Sea, *arriving from Creature Publishing in fall 2025.*

JOINER

I wipe the polished granite surface of the bar again with a damp white towel. I need something to do with my hands. It's been a quiet night—a few drinks earlier, burgers to go. Here and gone. I haven't said anything for several minutes. My tongue is a lead sinker in my mouth.

"I'm sure she's fine," says Tom Calvin, one of our regulars.

I jump a little. Refocus.

"Probably just got another job or something and didn't bother telling you all." He rolls his shoulders, cracks his neck. I think of the tiny gas bubbles around his spine, rising and popping like the ones in his beer glass. Pot lights over the bar pick up gray veins in his red hair. He runs his hand through it.

He's talking about Devon, another girl who tends bar at the Five Ponds Golf and Country Club here in northwest Georgia. She's been missing for the past two days.

I listen to the frogs outside. Their throaty, baritone calls carry in through the open window. "Maybe," I say, after a minute. Then my tongue sinks, settles again. I wipe the bar.

"She'll turn up," he says. He puts his hand over mine, and I let it rest there for a moment before pulling away. I put both my hands in my apron pockets for safe keeping. He folds his together. "I'll take another beer, by the way."

I think that another beer isn't by the way of anything. But I get him one and set it on the cardboard coaster in front of him.

§

Tom isn't a club member, but Five Ponds is open to the public. Anyone who's wearing khakis and a collared shirt is welcome. Tom, late thirties, tired but not yet old, wears that. He works as a sales representative for a beer company. I don't know when he finds time to actually work, though. My shifts start at three, and by then he's here, on his usual barstool or out on the deck. He never plays golf.

Tom and I are not having an affair, but lots of people think we are. His wife is one of them. I'm head bartender and I close most nights—more often this week than usual, since Devon's been gone. Tom stays until closing or just about, at least every night I work. At the bar, he sits right across from me, drinking so many Bud Light drafts that I often lose count. I usually charge him for twelve.

He tips well because he's trying to get me to have an affair with him.

Some nights his speech slurs and his blue eyes won't focus. Tries to stare at me but can't. Grabs my hand or my arm if I'm close enough. He usually only gets to "Rebecca, Rebecca *please*. Please, Rebecca." But I know what comes next. Sometimes he cries, but not so much that tears fall. Sometimes he just kicks his barstool and walks out onto the deck. Or leaves. Some nights I almost call after him, his name a pebble in my mouth I can't spit out.

§

Tonight is not one of those.

Nights like this one, Tom and I are something like friends. Or could be. Maybe more, if things were just a little different. But they aren't. And so we're here, like this, toes on a fault line that I won't cross but sometimes want to.

He's in a good mood, telling me about work and new accounts on his route. His laugh is deep and it bobs his Adam's apple above the tan line at his open collar. I like the sound of it.

A couple of the other regulars, Five Ponds members, were here earlier. Rod Harte and Dwayne Martins. Gone now, shamed home by wives. Not before Rod broke a beer mug and Dwayne threw up in the men's room. I picked up the glass, cutting my hand. Ignored the rest.

"Grab yourself a beer and put it on my tab. Come out on the deck," Tom calls to me. His voice is different now. Light and forced. I'm putting away dishes in the kitchen. Stack and clatter.

I do get a beer, but I don't charge him. Five Ponds can stand me a drink or two. Tom ducks beneath the doorframe and I follow him outside. He's over six feet tall and there's something clumsy about him. Limbs too loose in the joints. Worn elastic.

The deck, along with the bar, is on the second floor of the building. It overlooks the eighteenth green, which is surrounded by the biggest of the five ponds—the only one that isn't man made.

The pond is really more of a lake, though no one has ever measured how deep its middle is. Long ago it was a glacier, a giant mass of ice that carved through strata and bedding planes and then melted, making its home here. The golf course was built around it. The pros here call the eighteenth green an island green, but it's not an island. It's a peninsula that erosion will someday grind into sediment.

At night it seems gone already. I look down and there's just the waiting body of water, black and glinting. More tar than liquid. And all I hear are the frogs. There must be thousands of them. Just background noise unless I'm here by myself.

I'm here a lot by myself. Audience of one.

§

"What are you thinking about?" Tom asks me. He steps so close that his arm touches mine.

I'm looking at the pond, my elbows resting on the damp wooden railing. Goosebumps bloom on my skin. I push backward to sit in one of the painted rocking chairs, squeeze the clean dry towel wrapped around my left hand. My cut throbs and it feels good to trap the pain in my fist.

"The frogs," I say, my voice flat as shale. "How loud they are. At night it's just me and them."

Brreppup. Brreppup. Brreppup.

The first syllable is long, the second shorter. Abrupt. One frog's call is louder than the rest.

"You're talking to frogs now?" Tom turns and laughs. "Told you you were lonely."

I roll my eyes, impatience sparking like flint. "Not talking. Listening. And I'm not lonely."

The lie weights the air between us. He faces the water again.

I'm trying to think of how to change the subject when the phone rings inside. We both know it's Tom's wife calling the bar because he "forgot" his cell phone in his truck. I don't jump up to answer it. If the general manager of Five Ponds, Jeff, wanted to check on things, he'd call my cell phone. But that's been silent all night in the pocket of the black apron tied around my waist.

"Time to go!" Tom says. His voice is bright but his face doesn't match. We go in and he pays his tab. I feel the usual throb of relief and regret. But I also think of the closing chore list, what's not checked off yet. What I can skip, since it's me on again tomorrow, for a double.

Unless Devon turns up.

Tom pulls something out of his pocket, slaps it on the bar, and blows me a kiss. He leaves through the front door. I ignore his gesture and step closer to the bar, expecting the usual twenty-dollar bill. Instead I pick up a small box. It's plain white cardboard. I'm scared to open it, but do.

Inside is a cuff bracelet—silver with inlaid garnet, a mineral found in this region of Georgia. The Carroll County Garnet Mica Schist/Gneiss formation. A jeweler wouldn't pay a dollar for it. It's beautiful.

I was a geology major at UWG, before I lost focus and decided to take a semester off. That was over two years ago. Tom knows I love the rock composition here. The Valley and Ridge, the Blue Ridge, the Piedmont, and the Coastal Plain. We're at the base of the Blue Ridge, the southern tail of the Appalachians. Everywhere I go there's rock underneath me. Changed and shifted and smashed. Solid and fragile. Nothing's permanent.

The garnet found here isn't what you'd buy at a store—it's murky and opaque. Not much to look at. Even cut, it's more backyard rock than gemstone. But it's old—formed between the Precambrian and Paleozoic time periods. One of the things that puts this place on the geological map. That was a joke of my favorite professor's. Everywhere is on the geological map.

I used to ramble to Tom about what I learned in my classes. He'd even help me study sometimes. That was when I only worked here two or three nights a week. I can't believe he remembered.

I stop myself from trying it on. It must be custom made. Ridiculous that he gave me jewelry. If I wear it, it'll feel like agreeing to something. And I don't, I haven't. Not with the way things are. I drop the blood-smeared towel in the bin and cup the bracelet in that hand. The stone feels cool against the sting of my cut. I pour myself another beer and walk back out on the deck, to my place at the railing.

Brreppup. Brreppup. Brreppup.

I finish my beer too quickly and look down at the bracelet. It's not *that* special, is it? Just rock and metal. Tom's an asshole for giving it to me. I've told him no so many times, tried explaining. But he doesn't listen. Doesn't hear me.

Anger flares, hot on the back of my neck. Does he think he can buy me?

"Screw this," I say. To the frogs, to the piece of jewelry in my hand, to the black water. I wind my thin arm back and hurl the bracelet as far as I can into the dark pond. I hear it splash. The frogs stop calling for a few seconds.

Silence like a damp wool shawl.

I turn toward the doors, a quick step, then slower. Flush of anger spent, remorse creeps into the empty space. Tom's been telling me for months that I should go back to school. I'm almost twenty-eight, with no degree and no prospects.

Maybe the bracelet was a reminder, not a contract. I inhale then push out beer-laced breath. No matter now. The bracelet's gone, and I still have to close up. One more glance at the pond's stretching darkness and I'm back inside.

The tables near the bar are covered with full ashtrays and sticky rings of beer. I empty the ashtrays and wipe them out, clean the tables and vacuum. It's muggy. My polo shirt clings to my back and my legs ache.

I'm about to leave when I remember I haven't checked the deck for glasses or garbage. I don't want a text message from Jeff at six a.m., bitching.

Sticking my head out the door, I scan the high-tops. No glasses. I have to grab a few napkins from the deck floor, a full ashtray from the railing. There's a breeze coming off the pond that feels good on my forehead.

I look at my cheap watch. It's quarter to midnight, and I have to be back here by eight tomorrow. But all that's waiting for me is my shitbox apartment and a few dying spider plants. Here, there's the breeze, the slow pulse of the frogs' calls. I get another beer. Back outside, I sit in one of the rocking chairs, close my eyes, and stretch my sore legs. The frogs' steady chanting lulls me into a watery half-dream.

A mosquito bites my ankle, jerking me back to wakefulness. I open my eyes, surprised for a moment to find myself sitting on the deck, in a dry polo shirt and khakis. The cold air feels wrong on my clammy skin, and I hurry inside.

§

We're slammed and shorthanded. Still no Devon. She'd been acting weird for a while before she stopped coming in, but she started here months before I did and she'd never been a no-call no-show before this week. Jeff thinks it's drugs—in rural Georgia, meth is a big problem, and Devon had been spacey for weeks. Forgetting things. Staring outside at nothing. Leaving messes for the morning shift to clean up.

Then again, maybe she'd just had enough of the snobby members and all their demands. More than once I'd heard her bitching under her breath—"they won't shut the fuck up," "stop yelling at me," "why won't they leave me alone?" But we all feel like that, some days. Working here means nodding, smiling, and keeping your mouth shut.

The last night she worked she forgot to lock the door behind her and left her apron on the deck. It had money and her cell phone inside. Twenty-two bucks in small bills and quarters, a pre-paid Tracfone. Maybe she thinks Jeff will yell at her for quitting like that if she stops back in to grab it. I rolled it up and put it behind the cash register.

Because of her, we got a lecture last week about milking the clock. It took her hours to get out of here at night. That could have been the drugs. Or a guy? We aren't supposed to have visitors at work, but it happens.

I never heard Devon mention anyone, but she didn't have a car, so someone always dropped her off and picked her up. Not always the same car. Boyfriend? Maybe plural. More likely than drugs. Or just as.

I think the drugs rumor is unfair to Devon. But I don't offer the boyfriend theory to Jeff. He's mad and when he's mad I stay away from him. I didn't even argue when he mentioned the extra shifts.

There are a couple of new hires training—Tanya and Barb—but Jeff won't trust them to close. Tanya isn't even twenty-one yet and Barb's not very bright. So for now, at night, it's just me.

§

Fifteen hours here feels like two days. Bar-kitchen-dining room. The circuit is a blur. We've gone through a whole case of burgers, and I've had to run to the stockroom four times to get more beer. Thank God we don't sell bottles. No glass out on the golf course. Cans are heavy enough.

My arms ache and my calves are throbbing. I just want a hot shower and my pajamas, but I can't leave until I clean up and lock the doors.

Tom didn't come in tonight. Fine by me. Or at least mostly. I haven't decided what to say to him about the bracelet. If I'll say anything at all. Thinking about it spikes acid in my throat.

While I'm doing dishes, I slosh chicken wing sauce onto my white polo shirt. I try blotting at it with soda water, but the shirt's ruined.

I burn my right thumb when I clean the grill. The cut on my left hand won't close. I'm so tired I almost let myself cry. But it would waste time. I vacuum instead.

A discarded chicken wing bone gets stuck in the machine and stops up the bristles. I have to kneel on the floor and lay the vacuum on its side to pull the bone out.

I leave cleaning the deck for last. I walk outside and notice a few forgotten beer mugs on a high-top. I reach for them, but stop with my hand halfway there.

Lying next to one of the glasses in a small puddle of water is my bracelet, looking as pretty as it did in its cardboard box, the red-brown garnet wet and shining.

§

It's been two weeks and Devon hasn't shown up or called.

"Screw her then," Jeff said, and mailed out her last paycheck to the address on file.

It's not that he's an asshole. He's not even a bad boss.

But he's told me how many bartenders have left like that over the years—no notice, no contact afterward, here then not—and he's tired of it.

I don't get it myself. Five Ponds is an okay place to work. Better than a chain restaurant or dive bar, and I've done time in both. And why not give notice? It's just weird.

I close the bar almost every night now. Barb and Tanya cover mornings. I only see them for a few minutes at shift change.

Jeff closes himself on Sundays to give me a day off.

§

"One more, Rebecca."

That's a joke of Tom's. Or wishful thinking. He lets me use the same glass, though, which is nice. Saves dishes. Some of the members insist on clean, chilled mugs every time. Kings of the country club. Big swagger, small tips.

Smile and nod.

Tom didn't stay away long. A few days. He hasn't asked about the bracelet, even though I don't wear it. I didn't touch it the night I found it on the deck, but Barb saw it the next morning. She left it with a note by the register: *This must be yours. Found it outside. Pretty! What's that stone, tho?*

I wrapped the bracelet up in the note and shoved it behind a row of rocks glasses, catching my muddy brown eyes in the mirror above the bar.

I saw worry and looked away.

§

"Get a beer. Come out here with me," Tom says as he ducks beneath the door frame to go out onto the deck.

But I can't, because Dwayne and Rod are here. The minute I sat down they'd holler for another round. Dwayne's gray beard is stained yellow around his mouth from smoking. He lights cigars inside and throws tantrums if we tell him not to. Rod says he's from New York City but his accent can't be real. They're here together five nights a week.

Dwayne had me make him a basket of french fries. A good idea. He's drunk. But he keeps missing his mouth and smearing ketchup into his beard. For a few minutes I just watch. They wind down like animatronics running low on power until they're quiet, staring into their beer mugs. Figuring they're happy enough for now, I get a drink and head out to the deck. I prop open the door so I'll hear if they yell for me. Bartending is babysitting.

"Finally. Forget about those guys," Tom says. He pats the seat next to him on the two-person rocking chair. Instead I sit down at a high-top a few feet away, glance at the spot where I found my bracelet. Look out at the pond. Almost thank him, but my tongue feels too big for my mouth. He lights a cigarette.

Brreppup. Brreppup. Brreppup. Brrep-BEP-pup. Brrep-BEP-pup.

I walk over to the railing and peer out, but there's not much to see. Just marshy blackness, a dull shine on the water from the moon and the parking lot lights a few hundred feet away. Layers of shadows.

Brrep-BEP-pup! Brrep-BEP-pup!

They're so loud tonight.

"What's wrong with me? Why *not* me? Rebecca? Rebecca."

How long has he been talking?

I blink. Refocus.

"I'm sorry?"

"Don't be sorry. That doesn't mean anything, you say it so much. Are you seeing somebody? I mean you're here all the time, so how could you be? Just—"

"Tom." I cut him off, take a deep breath. Get ready to fumble through it— that he's married, that it's too complicated. Try to convince both of us.

But then there's a loud noise from inside, a bang and a shudder. I look behind me, into the bar. *Shit.*

Dwayne is lying on the floor next to his turned-over chair. French fries are strewn around him, ketchup glopped on the carpet. I think it's on his face until

I realize the smear over his right eye is blood. More blood on the corner of the table.

Rod stands over him laughing and singing his name.

"Christ," I mutter. I run over to Dwayne, grip his shoulder to shake him, then think that's a bad idea. Something about spine damage?

So I yell, "Dwayne! Wake up!" in his face while holding his head still.

He doesn't move, so I holler for Tom to get a bar towel and call 911. Rod is humming to himself. I hold the towel Tom brings to the gash in Dwayne's head and wait for the ambulance.

Shit shit shit. I consider calling Jeff but don't. It's late, and I'm not sure if I'd get in trouble. I don't think I did anything to cause this—they always drink this much—but I don't feel like explaining right now. He'll find out about it in the morning, anyway.

The paramedics insist that Rod comes with them. He's crouched on the floor rocking back and forth and won't respond to them or the flashlight they shine in his eyes. I tell the police officer, a short woman with a sharp nose, their full names and look up their home numbers on the pro shop computer. Let her contact their spouses. She looks hard at me, asks how many drinks I served them. I throw out a number we both know is too low and save my apologies for Jeff in the morning.

They leave and I lock the door behind them, turn around, survey the floor. I pick up the chair and move the table out. Toss the fries in the garbage. Wipe up the blobs of ketchup. Blot at the blood stain. Then I find some carpet cleaner and spray it on the dark spots, deciding it should soak for a few minutes.

I stand still in the middle of the room and embrace the quiet. I pour myself a beer and walk out onto the deck, planning to relax for a minute before scrubbing the carpet. But Tom is there, sitting in a rocking chair like all the questions I don't want to answer.

"I forgot you were here," I tell him. Too tired for hedging.

"You always do." He lights a cigarette.

"Thanks for your help with Dwayne."

"No problem. Hey, are you okay? Do you want me to stay while you close? I could see you home, too."

I collapse into a deck chair across from him. "See me home? Tom."

Brrep-bep-pup. Brrep-bep-pup.

"You know what I mean." He sets his empty beer mug down on the rocking chair's armrest, leaning forward to balance it there.

My body sags like it belongs to someone else. Limbs spent, rebelling. "I do. I always do. But—"

"My marriage is over. It's done."

"It's not. When it is, you'll get a divorce. That's what they're for. And then—"

"She'll never give me a divorce, not without a fight. It'll take forever. But we're both here right now."

I want to ask him why he won't stop pushing me. Or is it more of a pull? To tell him that some nights, even second place seems tempting. That my days don't feel done until I see him. And I sometimes hate him for that. But more often I hate myself. "Tom" is all I manage and it's not enough.

His face changes. Hardens. "You can be *such* a cold bitch, you know that?" He throws his shoulders back, huffs out something between a sigh and a cough. His beer mug falls, shatters near my feet on the wooden floor. For a moment he looks stricken, panicked.

I reach out to steady him, to argue, show him he's wrong. My hand gets halfway there, but I draw it back and fold both hands in my lap. I press my right thumb into my left palm until both healing injuries throb. The pain feels balanced.

"It's okay, Tom," I say, meaning the broken glass. Us.

Brreppup. Brrep-bep-pup. Brrep-bep-pup. Brrep-BEP-pup.

"No," he says, "no it's not," and stands to walk around the sharp mess. He throws his cigarette over the railing and his face is red—mad or embarrassed or about to cry, I can't tell. Wide wooden steps lead from the deck down to the cart path and the parking lot, and he stomps down them to where his truck is parked. He opens the driver's side door, gets in, and slams it. I don't know if he should drive. I don't try to stop him.

Looking down, I see a small shard of glass half embedded in my left ankle. It's not bleeding. I barely feel it. I look at it for a minute before pulling it out and flicking it toward the pond.

I should walk inside to get the broom and dustpan. I will. But the glass can wait, just like the carpet stains. I feel slow and heavy. Wet leaves in a weak breeze.

Brreppup. Brreppup. Brrep-bep-pup. Brreb-ep-pup. Breb-ep-puh. Breb-eccuh. Bre-becca.

I shake my head. I'm hearing things. Alone too much, like Tom says. I swallow most of my lukewarm beer and throw the dregs over the side of the railing, keeping my eyes on the pond until I hurry inside and shut the door hard behind me. I focus on the carpet and forget about the broken glass.

§

Jeff called me into his office early this afternoon and made me fill out an incident report. I wrote down exactly what happened with Dwayne and Rod last night, but left out that I was drinking a beer. When he asked me how many rounds they had, I answered "several." Jeff didn't yell at me. He just nodded and chewed his right thumbnail while I talked.

"Okay," Jeff said. "Next time clean up the glass you break." When he didn't move or say anything else I stood up, figuring I could go.

"Wait," he said. "Rebecca. Devon's mother called me today." He said it like he didn't want to tell me.

"What happened, then?"

"She called me looking for Devon. I told her she split on us about two weeks ago. That's around the last time her mom heard from her, too."

"Is something wrong, then? She's in trouble?" It came out angry, but I didn't know who I was mad at. Not Jeff. I stared at my feet.

"She's calling the police, but she said Devon goes off like this sometimes. They're not real close, her and Devon. It's more like a precaution. She thinks Devon'll show up soon. People can't just disappear, you know?"

Except that she did. And, according to him, others had, too.

I looked up. "Jeff, Devon and those other girls—the ones you thought quit with no notice. What if someone—"

"Stop. Don't talk about boogeymen. And don't mention any of this to the members. Do you want me to stay and close with you tonight? I don't want you to freak out and run off, too."

I thought about Devon's apron, her phone, how she never came back for them. I pictured her getting into a car she never made it out of. But Jeff has a new baby at home and I'd hate to pull him away from his family.

Besides, I figured Tom would be in. That things would be normal enough.

"I'll be fine," I said.

§

Dwayne hasn't left the hospital since he got there last night. He has a hairline skull fracture. Cracked it just right on the table. He'll be better soon, the doctors say, but they recommend that he stop drinking. He won't.

Rod was released to his wife after a couple hours of observation. I hear this all from the head golf pro before he leaves for the night. He doesn't say we're lucky no one is suing. He doesn't have to.

The door opens at eight o'clock, and I almost smile, thinking it's going to be Tom. I hope he forgot about what he said, what I didn't, that it can be a regular night. That we can talk about anything else but us.

Instead of Tom it's two police officers. One of them is the woman who was here last night. She looks at me the way she did then. As they come closer, I read their name tags and try not to look nervous. *O. Thompson*, and her partner, *O. Harding*.

I plaster on my waitress smile. There are a few customers in the bar, and I feel them staring. "How may I help you, officers?" I ask. "Is this about Dwayne again?"

"No, ma'am," says Officer Thompson. "This is about Devon Jankowski. You worked with her here?"

They continue to ask me similar questions. None of my answers seem helpful, though they both look up when I tell them about Devon's apron. I get it for them and they put it in a plastic bag that Officer Harding whips out of his back pocket. I also give them Devon's last time card.

They don't write much in their notebooks except the last date Devon worked and the time she punched in. She never punched out. They write down their names and phone numbers and give me the piece of paper.

They ask me to call them if I hear anything, either from her or about her. I think that goes without saying, but it's a good way to end a conversation like this. Their stay lasts less than fifteen minutes.

I give an early last call to the few customers who have gone back to their Braves game and get ready to close the place. They pay their tabs and leave. I clear their tables. Since it's been slow there's not much cleaning to do. The carpet's not very dirty and I skip vacuuming. I take my ring of work keys out of my apron and make the rounds, locking the kitchen door, the stockroom, the register.

It's not quite nine o'clock and I walk outside to watch the sun sink over the low hills of the golf course. It's beautiful, and I hardly ever get to see it. The bar is usually busy around this time. Golfers have to get off the course at dusk.

I stand at the railing for a long time, staring as the sky shifts from blue to orange to pink before settling on a blackish-purple. I can't make out the sixteenth or seventeenth tee box anymore, or the colored wooden markers. Even the huge metal maintenance shed on the far side of the parking lot dissolves in the darkness. I fiddle with my keys, twirling the ring around and around, running the teeth of each key against the pink new skin of my right thumb.

Then, from the pond, the first frog croaks. *Brreppup.*

Startled, I drop my keys over the railing. They clink on the cart path below me. "*Fuck.*" I won't be able to see shit down there.

I take my cell phone out of my apron pocket to use as a flashlight. Low battery. It doesn't help much, but the screen's weak glow lets me see enough to avoid tripping over a sand rake that someone left lying across the cart path.

The rest of the frogs have joined the first. I listen to them call from their positions on the bank and in the shallow water.

Brreppup. Brreppup. Brreppup.

They're so much louder now that I'm down here with them. I try to ignore the sound, but it's hard being this close.

Brreppup. Brreppup. Brreb-EP-pup. Brreb-EP-puh.

I keep my phone out, sweeping it along the ground in front of me, but I don't see my keys. I look up to the deck, trying to figure out exactly where I stood when I dropped them. I look back down, confused. They should be right in front of me. I heard them hit the concrete.

Brreb-EP-pup. Brreb-EP-puh.

I walk in circles, going farther out each time, keeping my eyes down and trying to hurry. Then, from the pond, I hear a little splash. I look that way, try to follow the sound, and see my keys. On the edge of the water. But a heavy ring of keys doesn't bounce.

Keeping one foot on the cart path, I lean over in a runner's stretch to snatch them with the tips of my fingers. The pond mud sucks at them. I have to pull harder than I expect. When I have them in my hand I run, leg muscles screaming, feet pounding up the wooden steps. I'm in my car, soaked in sweat and driving home too fast, less than three minutes later.

§

The bar has been packed all night. Some people still gossip about Devon, telling different made-up versions of what happened to her, asking me if I know any details. I don't. They look disappointed, but go on speculating. The drugs rumor has grown to a deal-gone-bad murder, hypothetical boyfriends are now hardened criminals. I don't argue but won't contribute.

I scurry around refilling empty beer mugs, dumping baskets full of greasy chicken bones in the trash can.

Smile and nod, I tell myself.

But even though I'm busy, even though I'm worrying about Devon, my thoughts return again to last night. My keys. How they got in the water. I linger every time I walk out to the deck, looking over the railing. Audience of one. The frogs chant in an even rhythm.

Brreb-ep-pup. Brreb-ep-puh. Brreb-EP-puh. Breb-EP-puh.

Tom doesn't show up for the second night in a row. I tell myself he's probably busy, that his wife is keeping him home. Every time I think his name I bite my tongue until it swells against my teeth. I spend the evening trying to focus on mugs of Budweiser, baskets of cheese fries. Not Tom. Not the frogs.

§

It takes me over an hour just to clean the kitchen. I spray, wipe, scrub until my fingers prune. My arm is tired from bricking the grill, and I decide I deserve a break. I take a bag of potato chips from behind the counter and don't pay for them. Plopping down at a dirty table, I look out the big windows toward the eighteenth green. I eat potato chips two at a time until the bag is empty, salt and vinegar burning my battered tongue.

I wish Tom were here, keeping me company like usual. It's too quiet tonight—like every sound I make echoes. I walk behind the bar and empty my tip jar, the metal coins ringing as they hit the counter. I cram wads of one-dollar bills and a handful of quarters into my apron, too lazy to cash them in for tens and fives.

I remember my bracelet. I reach over the rocks glasses and unwrap it. With the garnet cool against my palm, I wonder about fall registration deadlines, financial aid forms. Whether or not Professor Morgan is still head of the department, if there are any state park trips planned for the coming semester. If Tom will ever get a divorce.

I cuff the bracelet onto my left wrist and appreciate that it fits just right. Then I hold it up until the muddy stone catches the overhead lights.

I prop the door to the deck open, and I hear the frogs. The air rushing in feels damp but cool, smells like the pond. The sky is clear. Stars like spilled salt on a deep blue tablecloth. I think about getting a beer. I think about Tom, about feelings that change and shift. I get a rum and Diet Coke instead. Then I think about Devon's mother and splash in more liquor. I walk outside, lean against the railing to take the weight off my legs. The frogs get louder.

Brrep-bep-pup. Brrep-bep-pup. Brreb-EP-puh. Bre-BECC-uh. Bre-BECC-a.

The first swallow burns my tongue and throat and I set the glass down on the high-top next to me. I lean a little farther out, careful to hook my sneakered toe into the slats of the railing. I try to make out their small frog-shapes in the water, on the bank. I can't see anything.

Bre-BECC-uh! Bre-BECC-a! Bre-BECC-a!

Maybe I've been paying too much attention to them. It's been a long day. A long month, really. Stress can do these things, can't it? I still need to vacuum.

Bre-BECC-uh! Bre-BECC-a! BRE-BECC-A!

More of them pick up the chant. I look at my glass—it's still full. They're shouting. It's crazy. Or I'm crazy? But I wonder... I gulp down half my drink, breathe out alcohol fumes and indecision. No running away tonight.

I unhook my foot from the railing. My apron feels too heavy so I pull its bow loose, plunk it on the table. I head toward the stairs, take a few steps down. Stop. Listen. Audience of one.

Bre-becca!

I'm not imagining it. Devon didn't either. What about the others? All the quitters Jeff talks about? A heavy ring of keys doesn't bounce. I take a few more steps, get closer to hear better.

Bre-becca!

If Tom were here he'd laugh at me. He'd say a golfer or a groundskeeper found my bracelet. He'd say the only one calling my name was him.

Bre-becca!

But I'm sure now.

Rebecca!

I cross the cart path to the edge of the water.

§

The night is black. The parking lot light closest to the pond has gone out. The sky is overcast, no moon. No stars. A light breeze ripples the water's surface.

I see Tom on the deck. His back is to the glass doors and he's gripping the wooden railing. He looks unshaven. He looks tragic. Solid and fragile.

Beautiful, from down here. I think sadly about my bracelet, how it's somewhere at the bottom of the pond.

Too big, now.

Tom squashes out a cigarette, lights another. Exhaling a cloud of smoke, he leans over the railing and peers into the darkness. I would comfort him if I could.

I should have, before it came to this.

I sink lower in the water, dark eyes just above the surface. Watching him. I roll my shoulders, inhale, move my long legs in the silt beneath me.

My body feels cool, weightless. I creep forward a few inches, settle into the mud and algae along the bank. Stretch my tongue to taste the damp air.

I know the words and I'm ready to pick up the chant.

Tonight I'll call for him.

TUMBLING AFTER

It wasn't a *pail of water*, it was a *jailer's daughter*, but like most of women's history, especially women in love, our story was polished into something smooth, something pretty for children.

We weren't children. I was nineteen, she was twenty. Anna. Saying her name is like a cherry in my mouth, still.

Her dad found out, careful as we were, that August night in the barn—her hair against the summer hay, my fingers tangled in it. He saw the lantern, saw us before we heard him, and then there was the raging and cursing, lantern knocked over, bales alight, and our terrified flight into the woods. Up the hill.

Jack was a slack-mouthed stable boy, roused from his stupid sleep to stop us while Anna's father doused the flames, yelling after him to bring her home. She'd be straightened out, shut in her room until she broke. I'd be flogged or worse, corrupter that I was, taught a hard lesson in the brutish ways of men. Anna's father could only confine and punish. What did he know of love? Of loving?

We made it a mile before Jack caught up, flinging himself at Anna from the dark, clutching her cloak and wrapping a filthy arm around her perfect neck. She screamed and then choked, trying, I knew, to call my name: *Gillian*. How could I leave her? I turned back, found a branch, thick as a fence post and heavy. Creeping behind him I swung hard, every day of kneading dough and loading wagons preparing me for that awful moment.

Jack dropped like a stone in a well. His body slid backward, head busted open and eyes rolling up, moonlight glinting on empty whiteness. I kicked his dead hand away from my boot.

Anna struggled to her feet, sobbing words I couldn't make out. I threw down the branch and reached for her, and that's when I heard the barking. Her father had loosed the hunting dogs—we didn't have much time. They'd find Jack, find us, but I had a chance to save her. I kissed her and yelled, "Go," pushing her on, spinning us apart. I moved too fast for her to stop me. They could do their worst, but not to Anna—they couldn't have my love.

§

In my descent I did fall, more than once, on damp-slick moss and rocks I couldn't see. The hounds followed me as far as the river, where I crossed into the next county and lost them, though the rushing water almost did me in. Hiding and thieving, I circled back three days later, spying in windows and listening near stable doors.

§

They'd discovered Jack's body but Anna was missing, despite her father's furious search. I said a prayer of thanks and slipped away, back to the shadows of the woods.

§

I've lost count now of the years alone, but we'll find each other again, I know. There's more to our love than one life and what's next.

Some things men can't take.

HEY, STRANGER

Friday

Well, the first few times I saw him I didn't think anything of it. Assumed he was as real as you and me. You know, a place like this, like the Two Door, we get all kinds. And lonely men? Our specialty, no offense, Mister, right alongside the french toast and pecan bear claws.

More coffee? Another lemon for your water?

[…]

Sure. Like I was saying—

[…]

Yeah, I know there's only one door here. We used to have two when we were over on Second Street. Moved here six months ago, didn't see a point in changing the name. If it's not broke, don't break it, right?

[…]

Sugar packets? Sorry—behind the ketchup.

[…]

Right. So the first day I saw him, more than a month ago—actually it was just before *you* started coming in here, isn't that funny?—I had just come in for my regular morning shift and he was there at the counter.

Weird, only because I'm always the first one here, but I don't know all of Ed's friends—Ed's the owner—and I figured the guy was fixing something. Stuff around here is always breaking: the walk-in cooler, the ice machine, the pipes under the pot sink.

So I said, "Good morning," and walked on past him to get the kitchen set up. I can't remember for sure, but I think he grunted something back at me.

A few minutes later I walked back out, to get the coffee brewing—we always start with two pots of regular and one pot of decaf—and he was drinking a cup. Of coffee.

But see, I didn't *make* it yet—the coffee, and there was none on the burner. But maybe he brought it from home, I don't know. These senior citizens, they're on a budget. Money's tight—you should see some of the tips they leave. I'm talking nickels!

So I didn't say anything about the coffee. But I was curious about him. I'm a people person, you know. You have to be, in this business. And people, most of the time, people like you, they like talking to me.

[…]

Thank you! Well anyway the guy looked up at me when I walked over, and for a second I stopped. Just stood there with my apron half-tied, two steps away from the counter. You know why?

[…]

No, you don't really have to guess.

[…]

I know I asked, but it's just, like, a figure of speech. You're just supposed to say "Why?"

[…]

Okay well I stopped because of how sad he looked. Like, super sad, and maybe a little *off*, you know? His eyes were this real pale blue, like faded old jeans—come to think of it, there actually *was* something familiar about them, but I do meet a lot of new people, you know, and after a while everyone looks like someone—and his face had these deep lines in it.

He looked so tired. Not tired like me after a double shift, but tired like he'd been holding up the whole heavy world for three weeks straight.

I snapped out of it though; half a waitress's talents have to do with conversation, getting people to open up, and I said, because there was no one else around and like I told you I'm a curious person—

[…]

What?

[…]

Well, people person/curious person, same thing. I said, "So, sir. What's the matter?" Because I'm also very good at cheering people up.

I'm good at telling jokes. Do you know the one about how to catch a pink elephant?

[…]

Well it doesn't matter. I'll tell you some other time. It took him a while to answer me, when I said what's the matter, like he really thought about it, but then all he said was, "What's the matter with me might have something to do with what's the matter with you..." And then he got more upset, staring down at the counter.

And I wasn't just confused but also, I guess, a little ticked off, like sorry but I don't *have* a problem, and I was going to ask him what he meant but then I remembered I was precooking home fries, so I ran into the kitchen.

I flipped them and came back out, ready to give him a piece of my mind, because why did he say there was something wrong with *me*? I wasn't the one sitting there looking all *morose*.

[…]

What, you're surprised I know that word? Of course you are. Because you people are all the same. Strangers coming in here thinking they know me. Thinking I'm just a dumb diner waitress. But you know what?

[…]

I'll *tell* you what. I'm not stupid. And I've got other customers. Your bill is $7.86. Pay at the counter.

§

Monday

So the pancakes were that good, huh? Can't stay away? Well I'll let you in on a secret. We buy boxed pancake mix and add water. And the coffee? Folgers. Same as every other diner in town. Try Daisy's Café two blocks over.

Maybe their waitresses will be smart enough for you.

[…]

Alright, alright. You don't really have to *leave*. I start chasing customers away and Ed will be all over me like white on snow. I guess I'm just a little sensitive about that stuff—people thinking I'm not smart or whatever—because I'm back in school after so long. I feel self-conscious.

[…]

Well it's nice of you to ask. I'm taking classes at ECC, the community college here in town. Not full time—I have to work, but I figure if I go summers I can get my business degree by the end of next year. Not that someone who didn't go to college can't know words, by the way. Even before I went back, I picked up a lot of things from watching my stories—*General Hospital* and *All My Children* were my favorites—and I would always hear things like *vindictive* and *adulterous*, and from the looks on the people's faces and the way they slapped each other, I got what they meant, believe me you. I'm not home enough during the day to watch them anymore, but every once in a while—

[…]

My point? It's that you should be more open-minded. Back to breakfast, though. I really think you should try the french toast. It's not from a box, and it's delicious. With bacon.

[…]

Yeah? Great, lemme run this back.

§

Wednesday

You're lucky it's a slow morning. I have time to talk. And you know what I've noticed? You never tell me anything about you. I don't even know your name, though of course not everyone walks around with a nametag pinned to their dress like me!

Well not that you'd be in a dress, unless you wanted to, and I don't judge, different strokes on different folks, you know? But—

[…]

Well there you go trying to change the topic again. Fine, be mysterious if you want to, but at least tell me what to call you!

[…]

That's better. Hello, John. I'm Missy. But you already knew that! Coffee today? Lemon for your water?

[…]

Of course. Here you go.

[…]

Well sure he stopped in again. I told you, people like talking to me. His name is Butch, by the way. Though I don't know if that's, you know, the name his mom gave him. Found that out the second day. He was much more talkative that time.

He was there at the counter, drinking his mystery coffee, same as before. But when I said, "Good morning," he turned around, looked right at me, and said, "Good morning. It's me. Butch."

And I did a little curtsy, and said, "Missy. Pleased to meet you."

And he smiled. It was actually a little gruesome, but sweet, like he didn't remember how to smile and it took him a few seconds of twisting his face around before he got it right.

And he said, "I need to talk to you." Like I said, that's what I'm here for, but I heard the timer ring for the biscuits, and I ran in to grab them. I came back out and he was gone. Poof.

[…]

No, really. Poof. Just gone. Though I didn't know he could do that until pretty recently.

[…]

Disappear.

[…]

Well I was about to say! Because he's a ghost.

[…]

Listen! It took me a couple weeks to figure that out, of course. Because he wasn't see-through or shimmery or anything like that. In the movies they always glow, or zap in and out, things like that. In real life they're just people. Dead people, but people.

I was scared at first, but not as scared as I would have been if I'd have known right off the ball that he wasn't, well, living. Like by the time I realized it, well, he was already just Butch, you know?

And him being a ghost, well, it did explain a lot of things.

[…]

25

Don't be like that! You'll make me regret telling you. I don't just blab to every customer about my ghost friend, you know. Mostly, because it wouldn't be fair to Butch. But also, I don't want to get a reputation again, and really—

[…]

Well, I mean, you're being pretty judgy right now, John, and you don't even have all the facts.

[…]

Okay. Promise you believe me?

[…]

Thank you. Alright. I swear, I don't have any bolts loose. I'm not imagining him. When you see things or hear things, you start small. A whisper, voices, shadows around corners. You don't just go from zero to all-there, walking-talking old men. So it's not that.

[…]

That's what I thought of next, too. Sheesh. Give me some credit. And no. No near-death experiences, no new spooky house, no recently dead relatives. Just me, my life, like it's been for a while—walk to work, walk to classes, walk home, repeat—but now Butch is part of it, too. Not every day, but a lot, and I decided that's a good thing, even if he's a little odd, even for a ghost. Not that I know any other ghosts, though, actually.

[…]

Well why shouldn't I talk to him? If you think about it, everyone you know used to be someone you didn't know, until you *got* to know them, you know? Otherwise you couldn't know anyone.

[…]

Alright. It's nice of you to be worried or whatever, but I'm fine. Anyway, the next time he came in—I think it was the third time I saw him—I talked to him for a little while. I found out he used to be a bus driver, but I didn't know then, of course, that he didn't just mean "retired," that actually he'd been dead for a while.

He told me he had two kids, though they were grown and had moved south years ago, and a grandkid he never met.

[…]

Well because he died, I guess. Not the grandkid. Butch.

And I asked him about what he meant before, when he said there was something the matter with me. But he just shrugged it off like he didn't remember, sort of furrowed his eyebrows—that chimed a bell, too, but like I said, how can a girl remember every eyebrow she's seen?—and looked past me. Fiddled with his coffee cup.

Then he asked about me, what I was up to these days, and I told him about working here and going to college.

On that third day, I guess, is when we made friends.

[…]

Don't make fun. What are you, jealous?

[…]

Well that's what it seems like! You'll just have to accept that you're not the only one around here who likes to talk to me. Or that I like to talk to—and you glopped syrup on your shirt.

[…]

No—on your collar. Left side. Oops, sorry. Other left. Yep. You got it.

[…]

You're welcome. Anyway like the times before, I didn't hear him leave. Butch. He was gone when I came back from checking on the home fries. I remember thinking it was weird that I didn't hear the bells. See those sleigh bells on the door? They ring anytime a person goes in or out.

[…]

Yeah, I know that was a clue. But not a big one. He could have just been a quiet person, shutting the door gently. And what do I look like to you, a member of the Scooby gang?

[…]

Ha! Daphne had *red* hair and mine is like strawberry blonde, though to be honest it is *not* my natural color. And you, Mr. John, are a flatterer. Anyway, some other things I noticed, aside from the coffee he always seemed to have, was that he never ordered anything. Why sit in a diner every morning but not order food?

[…]

No, again, I don't want you to guess.

[…]

Well don't get mad! Jeez! Sorry.

[…]

Okay. I'll tell you why. Because when you're a ghost you don't need to eat real food. Or maybe they can't. Or they have a special food only they can eat, like vegans. I've never asked him.

But honestly, those things occurred to me later. The way I really found out was just like in the movies. I *asked* about him.

For a while, I'd meant to. To ask Ed—Ed's the owner, remember?—about his friend who's here in the mornings, if he's some kind of new night janitor or watchman or something. But Ed usually cooks for the late shift, and I'm always gone by three. I have evening classes at four, so I have to hustle out of here to make it on time.

[…]

Yep, at ECC! You have a good memory.

[…]

No, the guy who made your french toast is George. He's Ed's brother, actually, and his cooking is kind of hit or miss, but don't tell anyone I said that.

[…]

Thanks. Okay, so back to Butch. On payday, Ed gets here early. Like eleven or so. Butch had come and gone way before then—he only stays like five, ten minutes, and I remembered to talk to Ed.

So I went to his office, which is really just a closet in back with a desk in it, and I sat down. "Who's the guy here in the mornings?" I asked him. And he said, "What the heck are you talking about, Missy? I have paperwork to do, you know." Well except he didn't say "heck."

[…]

Yeah, Ed's kind of a grouch. But you get used to it. Then I said, "The guy here every morning. Butch. Why does he have a key? Does he fix stuff?" And he said, "You're the first one in, Miss. It's only you and Keisha have keys. Quit being squirrely."

[…]

Yeah, Keisha's here alone at night, sometimes—I open most days and she closes. Why are you asking about Keisha? Is it my turn to get jealous?

[…]

I was just kidding! Well, after that I described Butch. To Ed. His black and gray ponytail, plaid flannel jacket. Glasses. A cane made out of driftwood that's always leaning against an empty stool. Work pants and black sneakers. But nope, Ed said he didn't know him!

[…]

Well I was, and confused, too, but I didn't automatically think *ghost*. Would you have?

[…]

Oh, sorry. Let me get you a refill. Regular, right?

§

Thursday

Butch Butch Butch. That's all you ask me about lately. Butch, or my schedule, or my walking route, or—

[…]

Fine, but remember what curiosity did to the cat! And actually that saying is true, or at least it was for my cat Holly. That's a different topic though.

Anyway, no, with Butch, I thought homeless guy, or Old Timer's disease, some guy who knows how to pick locks. But he wasn't scary, and he seemed pretty not-homeless, and I've never heard of forgetful old folks breaking into diners just to chat with waitresses.

And if he were homeless wouldn't he want some food sometimes? But still, it was possible. A homeless lock-picking dementia sufferer. Poor guy, is how I really felt.

I wondered if I should explain it all to Ed so he'd know I wasn't nutty. About how Butch visits. But then I thought Ed might try to have him arrested for loitering or something. He would have been more ticked about Butch bringing his own coffee and not ordering food than he would have been ticked that someone was breaking and entering.

I decided to just ask Butch myself, you know? Not because I didn't like him here, actually I do like his company, quiet and like—companionable? Is that the word? But really, it was because I was kind of worried about him.

I thought, what if no one knew where he went those mornings? What if he wasn't supposed to be out walking around alone? I mean, there's traffic and Lord-knows-what out there. One time I even saw a street musician.

Well that was about a week and a half ago—not when I saw the street musician but when I talked to Ed, and I—whoops. When did those people walk in? Table of six. Hope they tip well. Listen, I gotta go. Your bill's $8.54.

[…]

Well, thank you for the offer, but you don't have to wait around, and I like walking to campus. I appreciate it, though! You're sweet to want to give me a ride.

[…]

Okay, well. See you soon?

[…]

§

Sunday

Hey there! You know, I think you're getting addicted to the Folgers. You're my most regular regular!

[…]

Oh, quit trying to butter me up. I'm not a biscuit! Ha! Come over and sit at the counter. On Sundays there are three of us, remember, so Charlene's got the section where you usually sit. We've got a 3-2-1 special today: Three pieces of sausage, two eggs, and one pancake for $5.95.

[…]

How do you want your eggs? Anything but over easy, because George will screw that up. Your best bet is scrambled. Coffee? Lemon for your water?

[…]

Okay, I'll just run this back and—shoot, I have to cut more lemons. Be back in a few!

§

Ouch! Got some lemon juice in a darn paper cut again. Doesn't that just always happen? Ooh that stings!

[…]

Oh, Butch? He's good. He seems to be struggling with something though. Sometimes he looks at me funny, like he's upset, but when I ask him what's bothering him, he says he doesn't know.

[…]

You're right! I *didn't* finish telling you about how I knew he was a ghost. So remember I said I asked Ed and he said he didn't know Butch? So the next time I saw Butch I asked him how he got in every morning. And he gave me the oddest look, like I had three heads, and he said, "My own two feet, Missy, along with my cane." And then he called me "daft," which I did have to look up later and which I did *not* appreciate.

But I kept pushing. I said, "The door's locked, though. I have the key." And *he* said, "Well where am I supposed to be? Where? Missy. Where am I supposed to be?"

Well I was getting frustrated at that point, thinking he was getting huffy with me, but I just took a deep breath, because I didn't want to argue with a poor old man, not that I would be mean or yell or like, throw him out into the cold, cruel world, because I'm not that kind of person, and—

[...]

Yes, I know it's almost May. You're missing the point. Anyway, I dropped that line of questioning since it wasn't helping. Oops! Gotta coffee that table. Be right back.

§

Lordy! These folks are going to run me off my feet today.

[...]

I'm getting to it! So I thought all night and tried something else the next time I saw him. I asked him where he lived. That way, I could tell if he was homeless or had Old Timer's. Hang on. I'll just grab your breakfast.

§

Here you go! Eat it while it's hot.

[...]

Well because if he was homeless he'd say "nowhere" or "everywhere" or something like that, and if he had dementia maybe he'd say the name of a rest home, or just "I don't know."

I knew he didn't live with his kids since they were down south, and he mentioned once that he was a widower. And if he gave me an apartment number, well maybe I could contact his family about how he shouldn't live alone on account of his wandering and breaking into the diner every day.

[…]

Well I didn't *think* about how I'd find his family. I would've come up with something later. Cross each road when you come to it, like the chicken.

[…]

The chicken who crossed the *road*, John!

[…]

Okay. Here's where it gets kind of like a movie, but not like *The Sixth Sense* or one of those. More like a Lifetime Original, some movie made for T.V. But even those scare me, when I'm watching them alone at night.

A couple days ago after I watched one I even convinced myself someone was prowling around outside my window! Footsteps and breathing and everything!

But then I said, "Missy, you are thirty-seven years old. Boogeymen aren't real. It was a dang raccoon." And I guess they like my trash because I heard it again last night.

[…]

Don't laugh! When you're a single woman you have to be careful, and actually raccoons can be pretty menacing, trust me. There was this one time, I was taking my trash out to the alley next to my place, and I think maybe there was shrimp in it? In the garbage. And I heard this weird clicking sound—

[…]

Nope, no dog. I did have a cat, Holly, but she died. I think it's because she got into my purse and ate a pack of gum. Like I was saying to you before, she was curious. About the gum. And she was a cat. So that's how I know the saying is true. Anyway, now it's just me.

[…]

Of course I keep my door locked! Anyway, Butch told me he lived at the end of Jackson Street. A blue house. He complained that he couldn't keep up with the lawn anymore and that the house was too big for him. He said he'd have to sell it soon, and that a development company had made offers in the past.

Well, Keisha lives near there, so I asked her, and you know what? There's a Big Lots on the end of Jackson. No blue house. But I still suspected dementia, so him not remembering where he lived didn't tell me anything. I had to try something different.

The next time I saw him I said, "Hey Butch. Where did you say you drove a school bus? The district, I mean."

He never did say, but it was a good way to ask. And he said "lots of places" but that he retired from Lakeshore.

So I called them, and that's how I found out he was dead.

[…]

Well because I said I was trying to track down a man named Butch who used to work there, because my mom said that a guy named Butch might be my real dad, which was a lie, because my dad's name was Joe and he always admitted I was his, at least in front of me, but I think people are generally pretty interested in who people's real dads are, I mean look at all the T.V. shows about it, so I thought it was a good story.

[…]

No, my dad is dead now too. But not a ghost, or at least I don't think so.

[…]

Well thank you. So, either way, it worked, and the man at the bus garage said sorry, there was a Butch Jacobson who worked there, but he died a few years back. Said they missed him, too, and that he was a good bus driver, though he got a little forgetful towards the end. That's why they got him to retire when he did—they didn't really trust him with a bus full of kids and what have you, too much to keep track of—and not long after that the heart attack got him.

Hang on. I gotta run some danishes over to table twelve. We're filling up with the church folks now.

[…]

I keep telling you, no! I don't need a ride. I like walking, especially when the weather's this nice. Thanks anyway, though. Really.

§

Monday

Hey, John! You're in late today. Busy morning? Or late night? Ha!

[…]

Just kidding. Okay. Lemme grab you some hot coffee and lemons for your water. Hang on.

§

Here you go.
[…]
I figured you'd ask! Where did I leave off last time?
[…]
Thanks. So you can imagine my shock. Remember? When the guy at the bus garage said Butch was dead. That was like a movie, too. I could've dropped the phone right there. I sat down on my kitchen chair so hard. Stared at the floor for a while, then talked sense to myself, like, "Okay, Missy, figure it out."
And I did. That's the day I ran up to the library and got those books.
[…]
Yes I got—oh! Before I forget, George burned the home fries this morning. Don't order those. What are you in the mood for?
[…]
John, you are fresher than this coffee! Alright. I'll surprise you.

§

Here you go. Don't let your toast get soggy. I had George use the raisin bread for something different.
[…]
That's right—the books. So at the library I checked out *Spooks and Specters,* and *Beyond This Life,* and *What's Haunting You?,* though that last one turned out to be a book on facing down the mistakes in your past, which actually I got a lot of answers from, but for different things.
The other books I got, though, the first two, they said that a ghost comes around because, one, the ghost is repeating some kind of pattern—
[…]
No, like I said, I'd never seen him here before that first time. Trust me, I know the regulars! Okay. So. Two, the ghost has unfinished business.
Well Butch never mentioned any of that, at least not to me. Three, the ghost is coming back to deliver an important message to a living friend or family member. But like I said, I couldn't place him.

Still, I thought maybe he did have business I just didn't know about, and then, early on, he *did* say he had to tell me something, though he never did, so maybe he was just confused. Or maybe he had a message from someone I knew? Something maybe another ghost told him?

[…]

Why would you think ghosts can't talk to each other? They're still people. Just dead ones. Oh! Four, the book said he could also be a demon entity that wants to take over my body for evil things. But I know that's not it.

[…]

I just do. You haven't met him. If you met him, you'd see. He's good.

[…]

Trust me! I'm a good judge of character. Just like with you!

[…]

Of course I do! But with Butch it's more like—oh, hey! There's Officer Jimmy! Actually he's our local police chief now. Got promoted. *Such* a nice guy. His younger sister Patty used to babysit me, and actually Holly, you know, my cat? The dead one that ate gum? She was his mother's cat Nancy's baby. I think there were six in that litter. I wonder if Nancy still has litters. Maybe I could get another kitten. Then again, Nancy's probably dead, too, by now. Do you think there are ghost cats?

Anyway, Jimmy, nice guy, like I said, I'll wave him over—

[…]

You have to go? You didn't even finish your breakfast. I was just gonna introduce you real quick—

[…]

Alright. Some other time, then. I'm guessing I can keep the change? Hey, I said—

[…]

Well. Bye to you too.

§

Thursday

Morning. Got a pot of Folgers here with your name on it. You ran off so quick last time I wasn't sure if you'd be back.

[…]

Well you're here now, so don't worry about it. Push your cup closer so I don't spill on you. It's hot!

[…]

Really. I mean it. It's fine. Say, want to hear something crazy? I saw a guy looks just like you last night after class, walking quick through the parking lot. I could have sworn it was you, and I tried to yell hello, but—

[…]

No? It was dark, anyway. And I guess there are tons of tall guys out there in baseball hats, right? But he had a beard like yours. Oh! We're out of the bear claws, in case you wanted one. We do have a fresh fruit salad, though. Or a southwest breakfast fajita. It's got cheese and chicken and peppers and onions in it, and it's served with salsa. Try it.

[…]

Aw! Well I did put my hair up different today, and this eyeshadow is new. It's Mary Kay's "Emerald Noir." Glamorous, huh? But you don't have to suck up, you know. I said I forgive you for running off the other day. Now lemme run this back. I've gotta restock tea bags and cut a few lemons, but I'll be back when I can.

§

Okay. I should have a few minutes. Want a warmup?

[…]

Okay. Where did I leave off? Oh yeah.

So I knew Butch was dead now, so he must be a ghost, and that made sense, what with not needing a key and not sounding the bells and always having his same cup of coffee. And then him not knowing his house was gone and what not, still talking like he lived there, no pun intended, and thinking everything was just business as normal.

And from the way he looked at me all funny when I asked him those questions—remember?—so from that I had a thought: He doesn't know he's dead, or he knew but forgot. Why else would he act like that? All confused. If you knew you were dead, wouldn't you say so when you made a new friend? Maybe not at first, but when you knew them better? Because it's bad manners to keep secrets like that. I mean, I've known Butch now for a while—a little longer than I've known you, remember, and he would have told me if he could.

So that explains it.

[…]

I wondered if I should tell him, too. But how would you take it? If you thought everything was fine, and then someone was like, "Just so you know, you're dead but I guess you don't know or forgot, and I guess I'm the only one who can see you and that's why you never want to try the pancakes?"

You see what I mean.

[…]

Well of *course* I still wanted to know why he was hanging around! But now everything was complicated, because how do you ask someone why they're haunting you when they don't even know that's what they're doing?

Though I have to say, I don't like to use the word "haunt." It's ugly, and it doesn't seem like that's what Butch does at all. He more just comes to hang out now and then.

Ugh. That old couple is back. Corner booth. Don't look now!

The lady will change her mind six times before getting a poached egg and rye toast, no butter, with a side of orange marmalade, and the guy will complain the coffee isn't hot enough. I better get over there.

§

Friday

There you are! I thought you weren't going to come in today, it got so late. I have big news! Plus, I was getting bored. The morning was super slow and tips were crummy. It's probably all the rain. But at least I get to leave soon. Plus, no classes tonight, so I just get to relax.

[…]

Oh—you don't want to drink what's in the pot. It's old. I'll brew some fresh. It'll only take a few minutes. Your coat is soaked—hang it over that chair so it can dry some.

§

Here we go. Nice and hot, so it will warm you up. Slide your cup closer.

[…]

Okay. Of course I'll spill it! The story. Not the coffee. Ha!

[…]

Okay. But first, backing up a little.

I tried to be sneaky. When I was trying to figure out why he was, you know, here? Like, jog his memory without letting him know I'm doing it, so his feelings wouldn't be hurt by the news of him not being alive anymore.

A couple days ago, I was like, "Butch. Is there something that you haven't done that you're just dying to finish?" I kicked myself for the words I used, but he didn't seem offended.

He said, "Just the gutters. Need to be cleaned soon. Hafta hire someone for it. Can't climb ladders anymore."

And he went back to looking at the counter. I tried again. "Butch. Do you ever get the feeling you want to tell me something? Like an important message?"

He looked at me like I was crazy for a second—he does that a lot, actually—but then he focused his watery eyes on my face and he said, "Yes."

Can you believe it? Oops! Forgot to take your order. There's some biscuits and gravy left if you're in the mood.

[…]

Yeah? Be right back.

§

Here you go. Try a little hot sauce on them.

[…]

Oh yeah, so, I nearly dropped the tray I was holding, when he said that.

And I said, "What, Butch? What's the message?" And he got all cloudy again. He said, "Sally. Sometimes you act whacky."

Well I got a little sick of it, then. Frustrated. I mean I thought I was getting somewhere, and then he just blanks out. Gets my name wrong, even. And I couldn't get him back on track.

But I didn't give up. The next time I saw him, I said, "Butch. Remember me? My name is Missy."

And he said "I know that. I know all the kids' names." And he sort of sat there scowling. I rolled my eyes at him, but I said, "Butch. You need to tell me something. Like, am I going to get a lot of money soon?"

[…]

Well you can't blame me for trying. But he just sat there, quiet. I said, "Is something bad going to happen?" And he cleared up again. He said, "Yes." And then I couldn't help it, I started crying. Because that's what I was really afraid of, to tell you the truth, that he was sent here to sort of *fetch* me, like he was a friendly, wrinkly, you know, the guy with the big curved knife?

[…]

Yep, the Grim Reaper. And then Butch, he teared up too, and I said to him that—

[…]

Well why shouldn't I worry about it? Would you ignore a ghost if he came to warn you about something?

[…]

You're right. I'm always here and what's safer than that? Anyway, that's the first day I saw him disappear, really act like a ghost. Like the crying was too much, mine or his. He just sort of wasn't there anymore.

And there was just, like, this sadness hanging over the place. It lasted for hours.

But *today*, today he was here, and he was very serious, and he said, "Missy. I remember." And I got excited.

"Missy, there was something you weren't supposed to do…" And I waited, ready. I thought he was going to say something like "Don't go on any airplanes" or "Don't eat foods that start with the letter M."

[…]

Well how are warnings supposed to sound? Anyway, he looked up, happy, and said, "Missy, I have to tell you. Don't talk to strangers." Well I laughed so hard I almost fell down.

I said, "Butch, how could I do my job? I mean, that's my *job*, Butch. How could I have talked to you? Or to any of my customers? Think again. It's got to be something else."

[…]

Well I was about to say, he got all testy, and said, "You want more advice? Fine. Zip up your jacket, get your hair out of your eyes and look both ways before you cross the street."

And for a second I forgot I was a lady, and I yelled, "Holy crap! Mr. Jake!" Because I remembered. I got it, when he said that.

[…]

Well I'm *telling* you why! See, when I was a kid I would never brush my hair or tie it up, really I must have looked like a ragamuffin, and I hated zipping my jacket, mostly because usually I would get my hair caught in the zipper and boy did *that* hurt, and I had this nice bus driver we all called Mr. Jake!

[…]

Short for *Jacobson*.

[…]

Because it was too long to say! Duh! And I never knew his first name.

[…]

Well he looked different then. Younger, sure—thirty years younger. Also no cane or ponytail back then. I had a new bus driver in fourth grade, so he must have changed districts by then. He told me he drove for lots of schools.

But that's what he said to me every day when he was *my* bus driver—zip my coat, get my hair out of my eyes, look both ways. I never listened, I guess it's lucky I never got hit by a car, really, but it was sweet that he didn't want me to get run over, right?

Then I almost hugged him. Mr. Jake—Butch. I didn't, because all the sudden I remembered that he was a ghost and I thought if I just hugged air, or cold jelly, or, like, mist, I'd freak out.

So I just stopped and was like, "I'm so happy to see you!" And then, after I knew who he was, I thought, well I better listen to him, so I said, "Okay, Mr. Jake. Butch. So that's it? There's nothing else?"

And he said, "What's that racket?" And he was right—I was so excited I hadn't heard the kitchen timer. There was black smoke coming out of the kitchen. So I ran in there to shut it off—

[…]

Oh yeah, real burned. Had to bake up a new batch. Anyway, I dumped the burnt biscuits in the sink, and I yelled, "Butch, don't go! Wait a second. I just have to ask you about what you said!"

[…]

Of course he was gone. It's like every time I run into the kitchen or turn my back, he leaves.

[…]

I know. It didn't make sense to me either. But don't make fun. I told you before, he's my friend. And now that I know he's here for a reason, maybe he can tell me more about what he meant. If he remembers next time he comes in. I'll try asking him.

Let's talk about something else, though. This topic is getting a little *morose*.

[…]

Well, it's a good word, right? Lemme clear your plate.

§

Another cup of coffee? You might as well. Sit here long enough and the rain might let up.

[…]

I think I need a cup, too. It's been a long day! There was all that excitement this morning with Butch, and then hardly any customers—I told you how this morning just *dragged*, plus I haven't been sleeping great.

Remember when I thought I heard someone but then I told myself it was a raccoon? I heard it again last night, and the night before that.

[…]

Yeah, I know. Raccoons or stray cats. But I got nervous and checked the locks and then I couldn't sleep. So I guess I'm just feeling kind of fried. Like bacon. Ha!

[…]

You know what? I will take a ride home today. Who would want to walk in this? Not me! I probably have another half hour or so, though. Is that okay? I have to cash out and do some sidework—wash the coffee pots, cut lemons, fill the ketchups. Oh, and stock napkins. I forgot to do that a couple days ago and Keisha was ticked. But I'll hurry.

[…]

Thanks! I do appreciate it, and—Hey!

[…]

Oh… nothing, I guess. I must be more tired than I thought. For a second there I could have sworn I saw Butch looking through the front window.

[…]

No, I guess not. Plus he's never shown up this late in the day, and I've never seen him outside. Like I said, I'm just tired. My eyes are doing tricks on me. I better get to my sidework.

Then I'll grab my purse and you can take me home!

§

Ooh, your car is so clean! It's like, new-car clean. It even smells bleachy! Not in a bad way, though. Just like, very fresh.

[…]

Well sure I like a man who keeps things tidy! Thanks again for driving me. This weather's only fit for frogs! I live about six blocks away. Quickest route to get there would be down Main, then turn on Third to get to Park, turn right, and it's near the end, almost to Seventh.

[…]

Ugh! Keisha's texting me, asking where I put the register key. I put it where I always put it! Where it goes! Lemme just text her. Sorry.

Okay. Now tell me more about you. Enough about me and Butch. We talk about me all the time.

[…]

Don't say that! I'm sure you're plenty interesting. What are your hobbies? What do you like to do, aside from visit me at the diner and ask about my ghost friend and—oh! You missed the turn. Hard to see in all this rain, huh?

That's okay, you can turn at the next block and we'll get to the same spot. The neighborhood is like a grid.

[…]

Right here—oh. You missed that one, too. That's okay. Next one, just turn—John! You need to turn, otherwise we won't—why are you looking at me like that?

[…]

Like *that*. John, what are you doing?

John. Slow down. Where are we going? Can you please turn at the next road?

John, I want to go home. You're scaring me. Please turn around.

[…]

Fine, just let me out. Please. Just stop the car. I can walk.

John, *stop*! Stop the car! I want to go back! What are you—

[…]

Hey! That's my phone! Why did you—

[…]

Don't touch me! Let *go* of me! John! Stop! Let go! I'm telling you right now! John, you don't want to do this. You don't. I promise. Oh Lord. Please. John, I'm warning you! You're gonna regret it—

[…]

You *will*! Ughh! *Stab*! *Stab*!

Oh. Oh God. John! Brake! Ditch, John! *Ditch*! Brake! Brake!

Oof! Ow! Ow…

§

Oh my God. Oh my God. Okay. Oh my God. I don't think I'm hurt. Okay. I'm okay. John, are you hurt?

[…]

Oh! That's right. I did. Well, sorry about that, but you are clearly *not* the person I thought you were! What even are you?! A kidnapper?! Plus I warned you.

[…]

That's not nice and you don't have to call names! I mean, you—ooh. You are *really* bleeding. I got you good, didn't I? Would you believe that was my first time ever stabbing anyone?

John, I said would you? Believe that? It's true. I think that's why I yelled "Stab! Stab!" Because saying it helped me do it and I thought we were friends and it's really hard to stab a friend, John, which I've never thought about before but I guess that's because you don't think you'll be—Oh God! Wait.

Is that even your name?

[…]

Well whoever you are, you made a mistake, like I said. And you know what? I just remembered I didn't wash this knife after cutting lemons with it. And I'm glad I didn't!

How does lemon juice feel in your stab holes, John?

Oh yeah. That's not your name. Well I'll keep calling you John I guess, if you won't tell me any different.

Ugh! Why am I even talking to you still? I guess it's because I'm used to talking to you. Usually you're a good listener. Are you listening, John? I'll tell you, I wasn't planning on stabbing you today. I swear I wasn't.

Then again, I didn't plan on you trying to speed off with me and throwing my phone out the window and then crashing into a ditch.

Anyway, I grabbed it right before we left. The lemon-cutting knife. Wanna know why?

John, I said wanna know why?

Because, I thought, well, what if it *was* Butch at the window? What if he was trying to tell me something again? What if I should have tried harder to listen to him before?

So I grabbed the knife and put it in my purse. Just in case. But I didn't expect to *use* it, you know? It's like when you grab an umbrella and it doesn't rain and then you just have to carry an umbrella around all day.

Though actually if I'd had an umbrella today I wouldn't have needed a ride so we wouldn't be here right now. Dang rain.

What I'm saying, though, is that those cuts have to really be stinging right now. Not that I feel bad for you. Because of the kidnapping. John?

[…]

Well look who remembered their manners. I'd help if I could, John. What are we even supposed to do now? Do you have a phone? John? And what was your plan, anyway? Lordy. We are in a *mess*.

Ouch. This seatbelt is kinda cutting into me, holding me at this angle. Oof, it is tight. The seatbelt. The buckle's jammed.

Do you think I could cut through it and crawl out the window? John? Then I could go for help. I'll just try to—shoot. Dropped the lemon knife and—nope. I can*not* reach it.

But don't worry. Someone will probably find us soon. Well maybe not. It is raining *really* hard. Not many cars on the road.

[…]

That noise you're making can't be good, right? John? You sound like a balloon with a leak. You should probably press on that. Slow the bleeding. I mean, I would press on it for you, but I overtrusted you before and look where *that* got me. It got me here.

In a ditch. Plus I don't think I can reach.

Oh my gosh. I can't *wait* to tell Butch about this. John? What do you think he'll say? Do you think he'll be all, like, "I told you so." I hope not.

But I mean, he might, you know? John? Or, crap. Maybe he won't come back now.

John, do you think he'll come back? I hope he does. I'd miss him if he didn't.

John? John? Oh. Shoot.

INFESTED

Viv noticed the first one about two months after she started therapy—a knee-high figure scrambling to hide behind the refrigerator.

It had pigtails. It wore tie-dye.

When she got up the nerve to look, it was gone, though she could hear it giggling. Maybe it had gotten into the walls, like that squirrel last fall.

The next one she saw was gawky and awkward—weird long arms dangling and knobby knees full of scabby, half-healed scrapes. It ran into the dark damp place beneath the cellar stairs and it would not come out though Viv tried to lure it with a trail of cheese doodles.

She really got worried when she spotted a third. This one was much bigger, and she recognized it from her goth phase. It scoffed and smirked. She chased it with a broom, but just when she thought she could shoo it out the back door, it juked left and ran upstairs. She heard the closet door slam.

It was probably going to burn incense and smoke clove cigarettes in there and Viv's clothes would stink like fermented hippies.

Afterward, a fourth showed, and then a fifth and a sixth, wearing all the bad hairstyles she'd ever tried, all the horrid clothes she'd thought could remake her—the miniskirts that left her ass hanging out and the baggy hoodies she wore like tents.

She lost count after twelve. They crept behind her and scattered when she whirled to face them. They skittered like roaches, hiding from the light. Sometimes she felt one breathing down the back of her neck, and if she gave it the satisfaction of screaming, it would run away laughing, shrieking "I got her!" in her own voice.

All those messy, wretched former selves Viv had tried to forget: the drunken one tripping over its own feet in the kitchen. The one that sobbed, all night, in the spare bedroom, so loud Viv couldn't sleep. She banged on the wall and that self banged back and cried louder, out of spite.

There was a violent one, too. Angry all the time. Its twisted face was almost unrecognizable as her own and it often pinched Viv so hard that blood blisters formed on her thighs and the backs of her arms. She begged it to stop, but it just laughed its mean laugh and sauntered away.

They became a bigger problem as days stretched to weeks. They ate her food and they used all her expensive shampoo. They spilled red wine on the carpet and stuck gum between the couch cushions. Rented X-rated pay-per-view movies and bought jewelry from the Home Shopping Network with her credit card. They pulled her hair and clung to her legs and mismatched all of her socks. They licked the doorknobs and chewed her shoes like hyper puppies.

She hated them and she wanted them gone.

§

Her therapist was no help. Dr. Agda. When Viv had told her about the infestation, she said, in her voice that was always an octave more chipper than called for: "The only way out is through, Vivian. You're doing the work, but it's a process."

And Viv said, "Okay," though she didn't really believe her, and they did another session, but that only brought another rogue self, this time from the future—bagged skin and age spots, muttering "Where is Thomas? Where is Thomas?" Viv didn't know anyone named Thomas.

So Viv cancelled her next appointment; she wouldn't invite more of those horrible things. She wouldn't make it worse. Already, her little house was overrun and she missed deadlines at work. When she forgot about an important meeting with a client company at the ad agency, her boss told her to take some time off. Viv said no. Her boss said it was forced vacation or suspension, her choice. Viv took the vacation days.

§

She tried poison first. She bought a dozen donuts and shook on some crystallized rat poison that blended in with the sprinkles. She left the box on the kitchen table, took a seat, and waited.

The toddler self came out from behind the fridge and sniffed the air. It clutched a raggedy stuffed elephant to its chest, and had dried snot on its shirt. At first, Viv thought, *do it, eat it, one down is one gone.*

And the little thing did reach for one, the biggest one with the most sprinkles, and it brought the donut closer to its mouth, but before it could take a bite, Viv slapped the tainted food out of the thing's tiny hand. It wailed and ran, retreating to its hidey hole.

Viv hung her head and cried. Then she straightened up and threw away the donuts, kicking the trash can after she banged the lid closed. She couldn't even kill one pesky little invader. She was soft. She was a coward and a quitter.

Disgusted, she went to bed. She didn't get up until well into the next afternoon.

§

She thought next of what people did when they wanted vermin gone, but didn't have the stomach to kill them.

Humane traps.

The local hardware store didn't sell anything big enough. Just little sizes to trap chipmunks and mice, the next size up for squirrels and groundhogs. But online, she found one made for trapping, among other things, "stray dogs, feral hogs, and bobcats." Viv paid for express delivery.

Two days later, the trap was set and ready in the living room, an open bottle of cabernet inside for bait. She would probably catch the drunk self first—she knew how much it liked red wine. It had the purple teeth and stained clothing to prove it.

To sweeten the pot, she added a Nirvana CD and a bag of peanut M&Ms. Then she ducked behind the couch.

But that space was already occupied. Viv found herself crouching next to her teen self, black lipstick smeared and crooked eyeliner making it look like a mime in the rain. That self used to light paper towel dispensers on fire in the school bathrooms with a shoplifted Zippo. It stole from classmates' lockers and threw the loot in the ditch behind the soccer field because it never really wanted what it took.

The teen self smirked. "Nice shirt," it said. "Makes you look like a cartoon bee."

Viv ignored it. She didn't point out that its ripped fishnets were clichéd. She just stared at her hands clasped over her knees, a knot in her stomach, wanting to catch one of the assholes and also not sure what she'd do with it if she did. Could she just set it free out by the airport? If she didn't take it far enough it would only find its way back.

Then came a loud click and snap and a howl of pain.

Viv jumped up. It was the sad one from upstairs—it'd tried to crawl just partway in, reaching for the goodies, and the trap had snapped closed on its ankle. Blood dripped; the thing howled again. Viv made the mistake of looking at its face: her at about twenty-five, probably just after Mike had left her. Its face was puffy, eyes tortured, wet orbs.

"Oh no," said Viv.

She got up and pried the trap open. The self that had gotten stuck there shuttled backward, but before it could hobble away, Viv said, "Wait." She reached in and got the M&Ms, handed them to that self, and tugged it toward the bathroom by its too-thin wrist.

She sat it down on the edge of the tub. She said, "Lemme see." The thing was scared, but it gave Viv its foot. Blood smeared onto Viv's pajama pants. "I'm sorry," said Viv. "I just don't know what to do. I'm sorry, okay? I'm just—sorry."

The self sitting on the tub kept crying and did not respond. Viv reached under the sink, rustled around, found antibiotic ointment and bandages. None was big enough, so she thought to make an anklet of six of them, stuck on perpendicular to the deep cut, making sure it was covered after she'd cleaned it with a soapy washcloth, satisfied it wouldn't get infected.

By the time she was done the self had stopped crying. Viv looked up from her first-aid job. The sad self was shoving M&Ms into its mouth by the handful, so many Viv was surprised it didn't choke. It held out the bag to her and shook it a little: an invitation. An offer.

"Thanks," said Viv, and took a few.

They sat together until they had polished off the bag. The self didn't talk, but Viv did.

"You're better off," she said, still chewing. "Really. Do you know who he married? His third cousin—Amber? We met her at a family reunion. I'm serious. And remember how much he talked about fantasy football? Like ALL the time. And he had that gross friend, Syd, who came over every weekend? The one whose ass crack always hung out. Please, don't be so sad. Not over him."

The self sitting on the edge of the tub was smiling by then, just a little, and Viv smiled back, and then she laughed, and that self laughed too, and just when tears pricked her eyes—because it was so stupid, who ever got sad about someone like Mike? It was so dumb—the self across from her faded, like fog in sunlight.

"No—" Viv said, but she didn't know why she said that, and she reached out to grab its hand, but her hand closed on the empty candy bag and she was alone in the bathroom.

"One down, then," Viv said, and she didn't know why she wasn't happier.

§

Back in the living room, she left the trap sprung and took the wine back. She chugged it from the bottle.

"Can I have some?" said the teen self, rising from behind the couch like a slow jack-in-the-box.

Viv looked at it for a moment. "Fine," she said. "But come here."

The teen self was hesitant, but made its way around the couch, skulking, until it sat down next to Viv.

Viv handed the bottle over. The teen self took a swig and tried not to cringe. It coughed.

"Easy," said Viv. "You don't need to impress me."

"I'm not trying to *impress* you," said the teen self. "I don't *care* what you think. Or what anyone else thinks. As if."

Viv sighed. She wanted to say, "Then why are you hiding your face behind all that makeup?" or "So tell me why you quit Debate Club," or "Give it up; I know your favorite color is blue," but she didn't, because she would sound like her mother, or worse, her grandmother.

So she said nothing. She just shrugged, and held out her hand. The teen self gave the bottle back, but narrowed its eyes.

"This whole place is so lame," said the teen self. "Do you know that? All of you are so fricking lame—like every single loser you ever turned out to be. Ugh. I hate it. I hate all of you."

It crossed its arms and flopped back onto the cushions.

"I know," Viv said. She looked at the teen self. She studied its dyed-black hair and its spike-stud earrings and jelly bracelets, and her heart did a sad flip. "I don't hate you, though."

She was surprised she said it, then surprised she meant it. She kept talking. "You're kinda screwed up, but I know you're just lonely. Dad left, Mom was always at work, and Grandma was pretty cranky most of the time."

"Right? *God*, so fricking cranky," said the teen self, rolling its eyes behind its chunky bangs. "Most of the time I fricking hate that wrinkly old bag, too."

As if on cue, the elderly self rambled into the living room, looking way too much like Grandma—it even had the same white-cloud hairstyle, and again, it called for Thomas in a wavering voice.

"Who the frick is Thomas?" muttered the teen self.

Viv shrugged again.

The elderly self turned to the teen self and reached out to cup its chin in a gentle grip. "I love your makeup," it said. Viv held her breath. It was the first time that one had mentioned anything other than Thomas. "Your hair too. So pretty."

"Um, thanks," said the teen self, and Viv wondered if it would smile. It didn't, of course, but it didn't pull away, either. "Who's Thomas?"

"Thomas! Oh you'll love Thomas. He's wonderful, isn't he?" It let go of the teen self's chin and looked to Viv, raising its wispy eyebrows.

"Absolutely," she said, playing along. "Thomas. Right. He's the best."

"I can't find him. I thought he was here. He's not though. Will you help me look?" This to the teen self.

The teen self glanced at Viv. Viv said nothing. Then it was the teen self's turn to shrug.

"Fine," it said, and stood up. "But he's definitely not here so let's go. I never wanted to be in this lame fricking place to begin with."

The senior citizen self took the teen self's hand, and the teen didn't let go or say "Ew."

"Thank you," the older self said. "I know he's got to be somewhere."

Viv watched them walk to the front door. The teen self looked back; the older self did not. The teen self opened the door. They stepped through.

Viv felt a vague panic clutch at her then. Who the heck *was* Thomas, anyway? Who the heck *will* he be? A person? A cat? She should have asked. And she should have told her teen self to try to get along with Grandma, at least sometimes, because when Grandma died its little goth self would be in ripped black tights in the front row at the funeral, sobbing the loudest of anyone. Viv got up and ran after them; she could call them back, say these things and ask these questions.

But by the time she ran through the open front door and stood on the top step, they were gone. After a moment of staring at the empty sidewalk, Viv closed the door. Then she opened it again and left it; maybe more of them would wander out on their own.

§

She found the drunk self sitting in the kitchen, gnawing on a stale hunk of sourdough bread.

"Want this?" Viv asked, offering the cabernet bottle. It was half empty.

"You don' want it?" the drunk self asked, looking suspicious. "Wha's wrong with it?"

"Nothing," said Viv, surprised. "I just… don't want any more. It's like, four p.m.?"

The drunk self spit a hunk of chewed bread onto the table.

"*It's four p.m.,*" that self mocked in a high-pitched voice. "So what. You're like, *judging* me?"

The word "judging" sounded like "shuching."

"No," said Viv.

The other self raised its eyebrows.

"Well actually, yes," admitted Viv. "A little." If she couldn't be honest with herself, who could she be honest with, anyway? "You threw up in the bathtub and I had to clean it. You barely eat. You're kind of a mess. And eventually you're going to realize booze isn't medicine. It's actually a depressant. You need *anti*depressants. And a sandwich."

The drunk self rolled its eyes and said, "Okay, Doctor Buzzkill."

"Gimme that," Viv said, and took away the stale bread. She threw it out, then looked in the fridge. There wasn't much, and certainly nothing she could use to make a sandwich, but she found a bowl of leftover macaroni and cheese and microwaved it. All the forks were dirty so she grabbed a spoon. Then she set it down in front of the drunk self and said "Eat."

"How old is this?" it asked, looking down at the dried-out, orange-ish noodles.

"Does it matter?" asked Viv.

"Guess not," said the drunk self, and it shoveled the leftovers into its mouth spoonful by spoonful. When the bowl was empty, it dropped the spoon on the table and belched, long and loud. Then it said, "Gotta whiz," and stood up, weaving toward the bathroom.

By its second step, its outlines fuzzed. It was transparent by its fourth step. In two more steps down the hallway, it was gone.

§

By then, of course, Viv understood. She couldn't chase them out or drive them away or banish them. She had to acknowledge them, even if she couldn't give them what they needed most.

Shaking off the fug of afternoon wine, she pulled the toddler self from behind the fridge and sat it on the counter. She wiped jam off its face. The toddler self pointed to a scrape on its elbow. Viv felt ridiculous but kissed it anyway. The toddler self jumped forward and Viv caught it, hugging it to her chest, putting her nose in its hair and inhaling the mingled scents of sweat and jam and baby lotion.

It melted away in her arms like wax beneath a lit candle wick.

Viv splashed her face with cold water, telling herself not to cry.

When she turned away, the angry one stood in front of her, its lip curled. Viv startled and tried to jump back, but she was already pressed against the sink. She felt the blood drain from her face. She had thought she could avoid this one for a little longer.

She was wrong.

"You want us gone that bad, do you?" it said, its eyes glittering with a dangerous intensity. "Fat fucking chance, you stupid bitch. You can't just kiss all our booboos better. We're not all gonna disappear just because you feed us some gross dogshit leftovers. If one of us is gonna leave, it's gonna be *you*."

Viv took a deep breath. "Stop it," she said. "Violence isn't gonna solve any—"

The angry self punched Viv in the stomach and laughed.

"Wrong," it said. "You're my problem, skank, and it just solved you."

Viv hunched over and slid to the floor. She squeezed her eyes shut and focused on breathing. She tried to think—where the hell did this mean self come from? She couldn't recall ever getting into fist fights—not at her drunkest, not at her saddest, not even as an angsty teenager.

"I don't recognize you," Viv said, coughing, looking up at her own face. She realized that sounded dumb. "I mean I don't *remember* you."

The other self reached down, grabbed the front of Viv's shirt and hauled her to her feet.

"You wouldn't, would you?" it said, spitting the words into Viv's face. "Always turning away. Always pushing me down, holding me back, boxing me up like something you can fucking forget. Well forget *this*."

It gripped a fistful of Viv's hair and pulled down, wrenching her head back. Tears pricked her eyes.

The other self yanked her forward and whispered in her ear, "I'm what you get when you swallow all that rage. *You* made me. Every time you wanted to scream and didn't. Every fucking time you wanted to blare your horn at someone in traffic, punch a hole in the wall, throw a shoe at your boss's head. Every time you just nodded and smiled instead, like the good little girl you think you need to be. I'm not *one of you*, you pathetic wimp. I *am* you."

Viv shuddered. The thing let her go.

"Get it now?" it said. "Or do you need me to show you again?"

"I get it," Viv said, and she did. She hauled her fist back and slammed it into that other self's face, and before it could recover or raise its own hands,

Viv hit it again, this time as an undercut to its jaw. Its teeth clacked together. Viv drove a knee into its groin, its stomach, its chest when it doubled over. She jammed an elbow into its back and landed on top of it on the kitchen floor.

The self beneath her moaned and gasped, and then it was laughing again.

"Finally," it wheezed, and Viv felt herself sink, falling through that other self like it was made of quicksand until it was just her, lying on the cold linoleum, knuckles bruised, elbow aching.

She lay there for a long time.

§

When Viv felt ready to move again, she approached them one by one. She hugged them or apologized or thanked them or told them not to worry, that haircut would grow out. She told one of them its stonewashed jeans were stylish, she brought aspirin and ginger ale to another that had a perpetual cold. The preteen one turned out to be the hardest; she peered beneath the cellar steps but couldn't find it.

She tried to remember herself as that self. What had she wanted? What had she needed?

Then a memory hit her, unpleasant as a swig of spoiled milk. Sixth grade. School dance. All the boys lined up on one side, girls on the other, only a few couples dancing to Mr. Big's "To Be With You" playing from speakers attached to the gym walls.

She had wished so fervently for someone to ask her to dance. A boy or a girl, as a friend or something else; she just wanted to sway along with another person under those rainbow lights.

But no one had asked her, and she hadn't been brave enough to ask anyone herself, and when her grandma picked her up an hour later and asked how it was, she said, "Fine," and smiled, then, in her room, played that Mr. Big song on repeat on her little CD player until she fell asleep, still in her pastel sundress.

That gave her an idea.

She pulled her phone out of her pocket, clicked open her music app, and typed in "Mr. Big." She tapped the second option, then turned up the volume.

"Come out," she said. "Come dance with me. Please?"

After a few tense seconds, the preteen self peeked out from the place Viv had just looked.

It opened its mouth, hesitated, and then said, "I like this song."

"Me too," said Viv. She smiled.

The preteen self walked toward her with nervous steps. Viv held out her hand; the preteen self took it. Soon they were swaying, the preteen self stepping on Viv's feet, both of them, Viv knew, picturing that sweaty gym and those rainbow lights.

When the song ended, Viv found herself swaying alone.

She closed her music app and went back upstairs.

§

She thought she'd dealt with them all but in her bathroom, she saw another—a tired one in a striped shirt. Bags under its eyes, unwashed hair.

Viv walked toward it and opened her mouth to say hello, but the other self opened its mouth too and Viv realized it wasn't another self, it was just herself—the here-and-now Vivian, all of her, and the only one left.

She searched the house one more time to be sure, but it was empty. She couldn't tell if she felt relieved or lonely or both.

Going back to the kitchen for a glass of water, she saw that the dry erase board stuck to the fridge was covered in penis drawings and her name scrawled in differing slants and sizes of her own handwriting.

A dish towel was lying on the floor; Viv picked it up and erased all the writing until the board was clean and white and blank.

Then she took the pen from its magnet holder and made a new list:

-Clean the house
-Take a shower
-Do laundry
-Go grocery shopping
-Call Dr. Agda

She put the marker back, straightened her posture, and got to work.

LOVESICK

When Steve's mom asked him on a Saturday afternoon to run to the grocery store for milk and pasta sauce, and to return her overdue self-help book to the library downtown, he'd muttered, "Fine. Not like I have anything better to do," and snatched the car keys from their hook in the kitchen—like it was her fault, somehow, that he had another month of boring summer days stretching ahead of him until football practice started.

All his friends—Hoser and Kyle and Mickey and Seth and D—were older than him by several months. They'd had their licenses since winter or spring and worked long hours at summer jobs. Hoser and Mickey at the amusement park two towns over. Seth at his uncle's farm. Kyle and D as lifeguards at the beach.

That left Steve, sixteen in late June, with a fresh driver's license and nowhere to go. Playing Xbox games and jerking off only filled so many hours of the day.

§

The three-mile drive into downtown only took about seven minutes. He parked crooked in the lot outside Super Saver's and didn't rush the errand. He roamed the aisles, spending too long selecting Ragu with Meat, squeezing a couple papayas he didn't buy, and adding a bag of Flamin' Hot Cheetos to his shopping basket. Then, on his way back to the dairy case, he saw Her.

Angela Tulley.

Siren of the Sophomore Class. (Kyle was into reading and he came up with that.) Steve's crush on her started in sixth grade, when her boobs grew before any other girl's. She had long wavy hair the color of Ritz crackers. Tan legs. Her shirt rode up to show her belly when she reached for the top shelf in her locker. She was the star of every fantasy Steve had, though she'd spoken to him exactly four times in the last four years.

And at that moment, she was bent over the eggs, opening cartons to check for breakage.

Now or never, he figured. He smoothed down the back of his short, messy hair, tried to memorize her ass at that angle, and walked to the dairy case. He cleared his throat.

"Hey Angela, what's up?" he said. "Buying eggs?" *Idiot*, he thought. That was so lame.

"Hi," she said, glancing up. "Uh, yeah…" Then she said, "Your zipper's down," grabbed a carton of eggs, and was gone.

So much for his big moment. Steve zipped the fly on his cargo shorts, closed his eyes, and leaned in toward the refrigerated groceries, letting cold air blast over his burning cheeks. He stood like that for about ten minutes, giving Angela enough time to check out and leave. He told himself he wouldn't see her until school started in September, and not much even then—she was in all the advanced classes, and Steve took the basic and remedial stuff. But that didn't make him feel like less of a jackass. Really, it just reminded him that there were several things he wasn't very good at.

He sighed, grabbed the wrong kind of milk, and left to finish his mom's errands.

§

The library was dim and cool, with only a few windows set high in its brick walls. A clerk stood behind the front desk, talking to a lady balancing a fat, drooling toddler on her hip. An old man dozed in a corner armchair, a newspaper open on his lap like a blanket.

Steve got in line behind the young mother, who had a hundred questions about story time. He had to pay a late fee on *Why 40 is Only the Beginning*. He'd just opened Snapchat on his phone when out from the stacks walked a girl he'd never seen.

Not a girl, really. A woman. She looked twenty, maybe older, and held three or four thick books tight to her stomach, pushing up her cleavage from a black tank top. Purple bra straps showed at her shoulders. Her short, dark hair was braided close to her scalp and a small rhinestone winked from the side of her nose.

When Steve realized that she realized he was staring, he turned back around and pretended to answer a text. But she tapped him on the shoulder.

"Hi," she said. "I'm Trinity." Then she surprised him again by holding out her hand.

He took it in his and gave it an awkward shake. He felt sweaty and weird.

"Steve. I'm Steve," he mumbled. "Hi."

He looked at the floor. At her cleavage. The floor again.

The mom in front of them asked the library clerk another question.

"Do you live here?" Trinity said.

He turned toward her. "At the library?"

"No," she said, rolling her eyes. "In town? I'm housesitting for my aunt for a few weeks. Just wondering what there is to do here."

"Oh, yeah, of course. In town. I live in town. But there's nothing to do here." He glanced at the clerk. "Unless you like story time."

She laughed at his joke and he relaxed.

"Well, I do like to read," she said. "How about you?"

"For sure," he lied. He'd almost failed sophomore English because he hadn't read any of the novels and was too lazy to even cheat off Hoser, but this girl didn't need to know any of that. He glanced down at the book in his hand. "Returning this for my mom, though. I'm not reading this."

"So you're not forty?" She smiled to show she was kidding. Her teeth were white and straight.

"Ha, no," he said. He didn't want to tell her how old he was, so he changed the subject. "What are you getting?"

She turned her stack of books sideways so he could read their spines. *The Modern Guide to Witchcraft. The Only Book of Wiccan Spells You'll Ever Need. Find Your Inner Love Goddess. Hot Hex: Sex Magic for Beginners.*

"Um, okay, cool. Yeah," he said.

Before he had to think of anything else to say, it was his turn at the desk. He handed over the book, waited for the clerk to scan it in, and paid the three-dollar fine.

He turned to leave and said, "See ya," to Trinity, hoping it sounded like he didn't care much either way.

"Counting on it," she said back.

Steve grinned and jogged to his mom's Sorrento. He knew he'd go to bed early that night. For the first time in years, Angela was about to be upstaged in his imagination.

§

Three long days later, Steve was able to borrow his mom's car for another visit to the library. He'd showered, brushed his teeth, spritzed on his Nautica Blue cologne, and put on a new pair of Nike joggers, layering his football hoodie over a fresh white t-shirt. Trinity probably wouldn't be there, he reasoned, but what if she was?

He could ask her if she wanted to go to the Dairy Queen down the street for a Blizzard. If she wasn't there, he'd probably go get a Blizzard anyway, then text his friends to see if anybody had time to play *Empire of Sin* on Xbox.

He walked in and felt the same cool air, saw the same darkened interior. The same clerk stood at the desk, this time typing something into the computer. She didn't look up. The same old guy slept in the corner. Steve looked around, even walking past the stacks, but no Trinity. He stopped at a display of John Grisham books, trying to be interested in their titles, when he heard "Psst!"

Trinity smiled at him from a doorway to his left. A sign above it read "Research Room." She crooked a finger at him. Steve dropped the book he was holding face down on the table and hurried over to her. She grabbed his elbow pulled him inside, then shut the heavy wooden door behind them with a sharp click.

"Hey," she said. "I knew you would be here today, so I waited."

"Really?" he said. He smiled and then quickly fixed his face to look bored, like girls were always hanging around for a chance to see him. "Cool. Well yeah I was going to get a book or something."

He looked down. She wore the same black tank top as before, with a studded denim mini skirt and black lace-up boots. She wasn't wearing a bra, and he could see her nipples poking forward. They made him think of jelly beans.

When he dragged his gaze back up, he saw a strange look on her face. Like she was measuring him—squinting a little, tilting her head to the side.

"Awesome," she said after a minute. "I've been doing a lot of reading, too."

Behind her, several open books lay spread across a desk, Post-its marking pages and a notebook full of small, dense handwriting. Steve thought they were the same books she'd held the other day, but he couldn't be sure. He tried to remember their titles. Something about a love goddess. Another about sex.

"Wanna help me study?" she asked.

"Study?" he repeated. "Um, sure. Is it, like, for a test or something?" He tried to imagine what kind of test she'd need sex books for. She was probably taking a college class. Were there tests on sex in college?

"Not a test..." she said and laughed. But not mean, like Angela. Not *at* him. "It's more of a tryout. For... a club. A group of women. Kind of like a sorority. You know how you have to, sort of, audition for them? And if you prove yourself, they let you in? It's pretty much like that."

Steve glanced at her clothes. "There are goth girl sororities?" he asked. He thought sororities were full of cheerleaders and prom queens. Not girls like Trinity.

"Yeah," she said, smiling. "That's a good way to put it—a goth girl sorority. Sit down."

There was only one chair, straight backed and wooden. "Okay," he said, and sat, rubbing his sweating palms on his pants and then letting them hang toward the floor.

"We'll have to share," she said. "Do you mind?"

Before he could answer she plopped onto his lap, wiggling like she needed to get comfortable. He tried to control his breathing.

"Am I too heavy?" she said, glancing behind her.

"No," he puffed out, then willed all his body parts to freeze.

She leaned forward and flipped a page. She made a note with a black pen topped with a pink puffball. She coughed.

"Steve?" she said. "Do you mind? It's just that these metal pieces dig into my thighs, you know?" And, again not waiting for him to answer, she flipped up the back of her skirt, settling down harder onto his lap, grinding against his crotch. He felt heat and dampness. The boner he'd been trying to avoid sprang up, straining harder, it seemed, for those few seconds of control. Why didn't he wear jeans?

He wanted to die.

Except she let out a little purring noise and rocked backward. "Steve," she said. "I think you like me." And she rocked forward and backward, then again.

His breath came in short exhalations. He closed his eyes. He couldn't speak. He didn't want her to stop. He'd never even touched a boob before. He'd kissed Karen Michaels in ninth grade behind the bleachers at a basketball game, but when he messaged her the next day she ignored him. Angela's tan belly flashed in his mind but then disappeared. He opened his eyes to see Trinity's face half turned toward him, a smirk on her lips. He raised his hands to cup her boobs over her shirt. He squeezed.

It was too much.

His dick spit up all over the inside of his sweatpants, once and then again, quick spasms shooting through his body. "Ugh! Ughh!" he groaned into the back of her neck, clamping down harder on her tits.

"Shhh," she whispered. "I got special permission to use this room." Then he felt cold air and opened his eyes. She stood in front of him, arms crossed, looking down.

He looked too. His pants were soaked, like he'd pissed himself.

"Sorry," he said, stammering the word again, "sorry, it's just that I—well I..." He didn't really know what to say. Had they just, sort of, had sex? Is this what it was like? It was amazing. Should he have worn a condom? He should have paid more attention in Health class.

"Oh, Steve. It's okay," she said, and smiled. "Was this the first time? I mean, with a girl?"

He didn't want to admit it. "Yeah, right," he said, forcing out a laugh. "First time? Not even close."

"Okay," she said. "Well, I have more research to do, so you should probably go. But I'm here a lot, you know?"

"Wait," he said. "Could I text you or something?"

"Mm, just stop by here again," she said. "That'll be easier."

He didn't think to ask why it would be easier. "Okay," he said. "Yeah, cool." Then he took off his hoodie and held it in front of him, hiding the wet spot.

She opened the door for him. When he tried to kiss her goodbye, she turned her face so his kiss landed on her cheek.

"Bye," she said. And she shut the door.

§

Steve drove to the library the next two days, twice on the second day, but no Trinity. He'd already jerked off about eight times to the memory of her wet vag rubbing on his dick, and told all his friends about it in detailed Snapchat messages. They didn't believe him but he didn't really care. At night, he dreamed of her, sighing and just out of reach, teasing him.

Then, the third day, a Friday, she was at the library, calling to him from the same Research Room doorway. This time she wore a dark purple dress that laced up the front, with the same boots, and again, no bra. As soon as he got through the door he sat down on the wooden chair.

"Did you miss me?" she asked, leaning back against the desk, bracing herself with her palms.

"Of course," he said. "Did you miss me?" He tried to make it sound sexy, but his voice cracked on the last word.

"Hmm," she said. "No. But I did think about you."

"Oh," he said, then figured that was close enough. "How's your research going?" He looked at her boobs.

"Pretty well," she said. "But it might take a while to gather all the… information I need. And the, um, materials." She raised her eyebrows. "That's where you come in. Wanna help me some more?"

"Like be your study buddy?" he asked, dropping his voice lower, keeping it steady this time. He was getting good at flirting, he thought.

"Something like that. Let's play Truth or Dare," she said. "But I get to pick."

"Okay," Steve said. He didn't know how that would help her study, but he didn't care. He would have said yes to anything.

"Tell me the truth," she said. "Are you a virgin?"

"Well," he said, and swallowed. "I mean, you and me, here the other day…"

"I'll take that as a yes," she said, and turned to make a note on her paper. "Your turn. Ask me."

"Truth or dare?"

"Dare."

He thought of how he might not get a chance like this again. "Alright." He took a deep breath. "I dare you to show me your tits."

"Fair's fair," she said, and unlaced her dress slowly while she stared at him. It fell open and she pulled it to the sides. Steve didn't know cup sizes, but Trinity's boobs were bigger than the papayas he'd felt up at the grocery store. He wondered if they were heavy.

"Can I touch them?" he asked.

"No," she said. "Now you. Truth. Would you say you've been in love before?"

He considered it, looking at her dark nipples, still on display. "I thought so," he said. "Her name's… Angela. But since the other day I kinda forgot about her. So I guess… I guess not."

"Good," she said, turning to make another note. "How do you feel about me?"

"I feel—I really like you. Like I *really* like you." Today he'd worn his cargo shorts again. The material was thicker but still, his body responded to her naked tits and his dick propped up the material at his crotch.

"Well, we'll have to do a little better than that," Trinity said. "Dare me to do something."

"Anything?"

"Almost anything."

Steve thought of how his friends would never buy that this happened. Seth bragged about watching pornos with his cousin and Mickey stole women's dirty swimsuits from the Lost and Found at work, but they'd never seen live tits up close.

"Um," he said. He wanted to make this count. "So… I've heard that girls like, jerk off? But like the girl version of it?"

"We do," Trinity said. "Do you want me to show you how that works, Steve?"

"Would you?" he asked.

"Beg me." She smiled.

"Please."

"Not good enough." Her smile was gone.

"Pretty please. Please show me."

"Better," she said, and reached under her dress. White cotton underwear dropped to the floor. She lifted herself to sit on the desk, pulled her skirt up so Steve could see everything, and closed her eyes.

§

He almost blacked out. He didn't know how much time passed while he watched, fixated, mouthbreathing, hands at his sides and dick in the air. When she shuddered and opened her eyes, he tried to gather the courage to ask her to sit on his lap again.

Maybe she'd let him pull his pants down. He'd even bought condoms at a CVS in the next town over and put one in his wallet, just in case. Maybe she'd put it on for him.

"I've got a condom," he blurted.

She laughed like he'd told a joke. "Steve!" she said. "You're so funny. But you should be going." She stood up and pulled her underwear on, then tightened the laces of her dress. She smoothed her skirt.

"The library's closing soon, and I've got to add a few things to my notes."

"Oh, okay," he said, trying not to sound disappointed. He realized he'd only worn a t-shirt, and had nothing to hide his boner.

She seemed to read his mind. "Don't worry," she said. "No one will even notice. I'll see you later, okay?"

"When?" he asked.

"Oh, you'll just have to come looking for me," she said. She was already sitting down, reaching for her pen. "And when you find me, tell me how much you missed me. If you missed me more or less than last time." Then she turned away, toward her books.

§

Girls flirted weird, Steve thought, walking away. Before he could get to the front doors of the library, though, the man in the corner woke up, his eyes widening as they rested on Steve's crotch. Then the man glanced toward the Research Room, looked back at Steve, and winked.

Steve grabbed a flier about story time and used it to cover his shame, shouldered the door open, and jogged to the car.

As he buckled his seatbelt he realized tears had built up, hot and stinging, behind his eyelids. He didn't know why. When he got home he ran up to his room to take care of himself, getting the job done with quick, angry strokes that left his junk raw. Then he let his consciousness fall away, sinking into a sweaty afternoon nap, and in his sleep he dreamed of Trinity's body but not her face.

It was half fantasy, half nightmare; Trinity's breasts were almost liquid and flowed into his mouth, one then the other then both together, choking him, her nipples tiny knives that scraped the back of his throat. Right when he thought, in the dream, that he'd die, he woke up, a spasm at his groin telling him he'd just painted his cotton NFL sheets. He felt disoriented and a little scared, and headed to the shower to try to wash it all away.

§

But the dream was still fresh in his mind the next day, and he didn't go to the library. In the shower that afternoon he tried to think of Angela, but his dick didn't respond like it used to. It hung limp between his thighs. He was probably just tired, he figured.

He spent the evening playing video games and watching YouTube. He told himself he wouldn't go to the library again—that Trinity was a freaky goth and he was a jock and it was a bad idea even if she was sexy and older and made his cock swell up.

He wasn't even sure if she liked him back. Was this how he'd always feel, when it came to girls? Confused and small and a little nauseous?

§

But his resolve only lasted four days. He went back to the library. And in the doorway of the Research Room stood Trinity, hands on her hips, in a leather skirt and a red top ripped low at the neck. She had on purple lipstick and the same black boots. She looked like she was waiting for him.

There were no other patrons in the library. No clerk at the desk. The usual dozing man wasn't even there. It was like everyone had been zapped away; Steve and Trinity had the place to themselves.

"Where are the people?" Steve asked. It was exciting to be with her all alone. But eerie too. Something about the air felt crackly, like he was trapped inside radio static.

"Slow day?" she said, and shrugged.

"But the lady at the desk…"

"I convinced her she deserved a little break. I'm getting better at that, don't you think? Steve?" Her voice sounded far away.

He moved closer to her. "Better at what?"

"Convincing people."

"I guess," he said, looking around again. He got the feeling he should leave. She hadn't invited him into the room yet. He could say he had to go. Make up an excuse.

"Steve," she said. He looked back at her. "Have you been avoiding me?" She puffed out her bottom lip in a fake pout. He glanced toward the doors.

"*Steve*," she said again. "Look." She turned to the side and lifted the edge of her skirt, showing him the lacy edge of her underwear. "I asked if you've been avoiding me." She let her skirt fall back into place.

"No," he lied, keeping his eyes on her legs. How would he tell her about his dream? The same one he'd had later that night, after the first time, and the night after that? That it was getting wilder the more he had it, her body spreading around him like water, but thicker, and he couldn't move, like he was being strangled, but each time he woke up coming hard into his twisted blankets? That when he tried to jerk off he couldn't finish unless he thought of her, and that dream, and it made him feel stupid and helpless and dirty?

"Good," she said. She pulled him into the room and shut the door. "But just in case, I thought I would do something nice for you today."

He swallowed and looked at her face. He'd thought her eyes were blue, but the color was closer to turquoise. "Cool," he said. "Like what?"

"Something special. Sit down."

Steve sat, trying to ignore the twisting in his stomach. Today he wore jeans and a hoodie over his favorite band t-shirt. The condom was still inside his wallet, in his back pocket. Maybe he would get to use it.

Trinity flipped a switch to turn off the overhead light. A reading lamp on the desk glowed behind its green shade, illuminating the small space with a murky, underwater glimmer. Steve could make out her usual stack of books on the desk, an empty water bottle, a crocheted purse, the puffball pen.

Then his attention went back to Trinity, who moved to stand in front of him, gliding her hips back and forth. She raised her arms over her head, dancing slowly without music. Steve stared, hypnotized. Then she pulled her shirt off, throwing it onto the desk behind her. She dropped her skirt. Turning around, she gave him an eyeful of her black lace underwear, backing up until her ass was inches from his face. Her smooth skin reflected the green light. Tattoos scrawled across her lower back, strange shapes in black ink.

"Do you like this?" she asked, still moving.

"Yes," he said. He felt hot and cold. He sweated and shivered.

"Do you *love* this?" she asked, a hard edge to her voice.

"Yeah," Steve said. "Yes. I love it." His breathing was quick, desperate. Like he'd just done sprints in football practice. Like he couldn't gulp down enough air. And he was so thirsty.

Trinity turned around and leaned toward his face, pushing up her cleavage to cup his chin. Instinctively, he moved his mouth to one of her nipples and sucked.

"Do you love *me*?" she asked, her mouth close to his ear.

"Mm-hmm," he said, sucking harder.

She pulled back to give him her other nipple. "Tell me," she said. "Tell me how much. Tell me you missed me."

He stopped long enough to say, "I love you" and latched on again, reaching forward to take her ass in both hands. "So much," he mumbled, "so hard." His whole body was parched. His throat ached.

"I thought so," she said. She whispered some words he couldn't make out. Then she said, louder, "You've been perfect for this. Just what I needed. Thank you."

His chest felt like it was going to burst open. She said she needed him. That was like love, right? "Do you love me too?" he asked, his words rushed, not letting her nipple get too far away. "Are we going to have sex? It's all I think about, please. Please at least touch it."

"Of course," she said, and he didn't know which question she was answering. "I need to, anyway, for this to work." That word again. *Need*. It made him feel big, like a man.

Then she was kneeling in front of him, unzipping his jeans. She pulled his throbbing cock out, tugged it a couple of times like she was testing its strength, and put it in her mouth. Steve whimpered. It felt so good it almost hurt. Then he was back in the dream, Trinity pooling around him, sharp and fluid at once, burning and cooling, thrusting and pulling back.

She had stopped. "Wait," she said, sounding muffled. "Don't waste it." Then she took him in her mouth again, stroking the length of his shaft with her tongue—slowly, slowly—and gripping its base in her warm hand.

"I can't hold on," he told her, his voice high pitched, needy. "I can't I'm gonna—"

Then he felt something hard against his tip and he thought it was her teeth, and he came like a showerhead on full blast, a sob bubbling out of his throat and tears on his cheeks. He opened his eyes to see Trinity holding the empty water bottle to his dick, squeezing out his last drops of cum like she was draining a garden hose, shaking it dry.

"What the fuck?" he said, too distracted to be embarrassed that he'd cried.

"That should do it," she said. "Thank you, Steve." She stood up and capped the water bottle, slipping it into her purse. She leaned forward and licked a tear off his cheek. "Mm. Bonus," she said.

Then, without looking at him, she picked her clothes up and put them back on. She stacked her books and turned on the overhead light.

"What are you doing?" he said. "Why did you do that?"

"You said you wanted to help me, Steve," she said. "And you did. Now I really have to go. But this has been great."

"Wait!" said Steve. "Has been?" His dick was still exposed, shrinking now and curling against his thigh. "But I thought this meant we were, like… We were…"

She stopped. Smiled. "Together? Hmm," she said. "No. But we each got what we wanted, right? So it's a happy ending." Then she opened the door and walked out, leaving him to jump up, turn away, and zip his pants.

By the time he left the room a moment later she was gone.

The library was back to normal, no static in the air. The usual clerk scribbled on paper behind the desk and the man slept in the corner. A lady spun the rack of romance novels while two kids lounged on beanbag chairs, reading picture books.

No one looked at him as he ran to the doors and outside, scanning up and down the empty street.

§

Two weeks later football practice started. Steve's coach complained because he'd lost weight—more than ten pounds since last season. His cheeks looked hollow and the skin beneath his eyes sagged.

He didn't sleep much, but when he did he dreamed of Trinity, of her body entering his, penetrating him, her flesh pouring down his throat, into his nose and ears, probing all of his cavities until he was drowning in her, strangling, pulled down by an undertow.

He always awoke the same way. Messing his sheets. Coming hard, violent and straining. He felt dehydrated no matter how much water he drank. Dry skin flaked from his elbows, knees, the bottoms of his feet.

He went to the library every day. Trinity was never there. The Research Room stayed empty and dark. It still smelled like sex.

He took to driving around town, hoping he'd see her. He missed practices. He checked two other libraries in neighboring towns. No Trinity.

He missed more practices, got benched. His friends got tired of asking him what was wrong.

He tried to sleep. He dreamed of Trinity. He tried not to sleep. He got kicked off the team. He drove around. He looked for Trinity.

He looked for Trinity. He dreamed of Trinity. He came in his sheets. He chugged water. He lost weight. His skin flaked. He looked for Trinity.

He dreamed of Trinity.

He looked for Trinity.

He dreamed of Trinity.

BAIT & SWITCH

"Fortunes, ten dollars," the jeweled crone had croaked. "Your future awaits. Take my hands; you'll see."

Her palms were soft—you still remember that—like gift bag tissue reused too many times.

You followed her into a striped, stained tent, where flaring candles made shadows move. A solid glass ball, murky with age, reflected your face like a funhouse mirror.

The cliché almost made you laugh; like an old movie set, come to life.

You sat, expecting plans you'd already made: graduation, a wedding. A baby, maybe two; but it wasn't to be.

Her gnarled fingers flipped cards face up: a darker fate. Malformed figures with pained expressions and bent, twisted limbs.

A tower. A tree.

Her guttural voice, low and scraping, slow, chanting words in Polish or Czech.

Then there was nothing.

Then there was this: Her gone. You, her.

§

A decade at least, maybe more, has passed, but still you call from the striped, dirty tent.

New towns, same promise: "Fortunes, ten dollars."

You wait and you hope, your voice wearing thin, for just the right someone to take your soft hands.

A BARGAIN AT TWICE THE PRICE

    If you had known Beth would leave two months after the closing date, you never would have bought the shoebox starter home on Oak View Drive in a sleepy commuter town with one shitty pizza joint and two convenience stores and nothing to do on weeknights but hang out at the rat-hole townie bar drinking too much bottom-shelf whiskey.

    If you had known Beth would find you so utterly lacking as a man and a human and a partner, that she would look at you with such disappointment that shame would rush down to the soles of your feet and back up to the roots of your red hair, you never would have proposed on that trip to the Keys with the ring you bought with your third-to-last paycheck from the cable company that would soon lay you off due to "unforeseeable market shifts."

    You were a customer service agent. Now you're a chump, and according to Beth, an alcoholic.

    If you had known all that and more, you wouldn't be sitting shirtless and hungover on your tiny front porch in pajama pants, drinking your fourth cup of black coffee, watching Tim across the street water his half-dead lawn for the third day in a row. You wouldn't be hoping for someone to walk down the sidewalk with a dog or two, maybe a fugly baby, just to have something interesting to look at.

But you didn't know, so here you are, tits out, and Tim just waved so you raise your coffee cup in an oddly formal salute and get ready for the nothingness of the day to settle into your bones like a damp chill.

§

You call Beth a lot. Sometimes twice a week, sometimes more. She doesn't answer. You leave messages. Last night, at the sound of the beep, you said, "Five years of talking every day is too long to talk every day and then stop talking every day, Beth. Dammit. Beth."

You hope she knew what you meant. That she even listened to the message. Maybe you should leave her another one later today, you think.

Just in case.

§

The Help Wanted section of the local paper is a joke—ten listings most weekends, half of them for babysitting gigs. You are not good with children, which is one of your faults, also according to Beth. "You don't know how to nurture," she'd said, and you didn't bother to argue.

At first glance, today's paper seems like more of the same shit. Your eyes wander to the window, not really seeing anything until a flash of red catches your attention. It's a cardinal the color of Beth's favorite nail polish, hopping branch to branch in the yellow-blooming shrub in your side yard. It flaps its wings like a signal and looks right at you, one beady black eye returning your stupid slack-mouthed gaze. It flaps its wings again, juts its beak.

"Fuck you," you say to the bird. It puffs its chest like it's better than you. "Fuck you and fuck every one of your goddamn feathers!" You're kind of yelling now, maybe still a little drunk, and you stand up to shake your fist, knocking over the dregs of a cold cup of coffee. The liquid spills across the newspaper. You look down, and that's when you see it.

The ad is in bold print, and so brief that it feels like a message from the universe, or at least a fortune cookie platitude. You look back up. The cardinal fixes its eye on you again and then flies away. You sit and read.

Landscape worker needed. Must have truck. There is a phone number.

Except you don't have a truck, so it's another dead end. You have an aging Corolla, because Beth drove the Subaru and she took that with her when she left. You were going to replace your car this summer, when you two got caught up on a few bills, but Beth had wanted the new counters in the kitchen and then the job thing happened.

§

A day later, though, when you glance away from Tim and his garden hose, you see that shithead cardinal again, perched on top of a 90s model Chevy pickup parked next door. The bird flaps its wings, pins you with that smug look. You give it the finger. It seems to square its bird shoulders and whistles back at you.

The truck is two-tone green with rust on the back, "Make offer" written in shaky script on a sign taped to the windshield. You glance back at the bird and it flies away.

The old lady who lives there is named Caroline. You've seen her get the mail and take her trash out on Wednesday nights. She's hunched over and probably weighs less than a fart. Tim told you her husband died before you moved to the neighborhood, that she's on her own now.

Cursing the bird under your breath and also yourself for being a moron who listens to birds, you go inside your house, set your coffee cup in the sink, and put on a shirt. Then you head next door to knock on Caroline's door with a fluttering in your gut that you can't place.

She opens it seconds later, peering up through wavy blonde-gray hair. Her eyes are a faded green. "Yes?" she says.

You tell her your name is Sean, and that you recently moved in next door, but of course she already knows that last part. She nods. You stammer and apologize and say you couldn't help but notice the truck for sale, then wonder why you have to make everything so fucking awkward.

"It was my husband's," Caroline says, not seeming to mind that you're an idiot. She has one hand on the doorknob like she needs it for balance.

"Skip's. It's been sitting in the garage, in the way. I can't drive it. Nowhere to go anyway."

You strain to catch all this because her voice is thin and reedy.

"I'm interested," you say, and try to guess how terrible of a person you are if you lowball an old woman, and then you think maybe that just confirms what Beth said, about how you're basically selfish and basically immature, and how you can't go through life not wanting to contribute to the greater good, or some crap like that.

You wait for Caroline to respond, to name a price so high that it will kill this whole stupid idea. She doesn't, so you throw out a number that is half of what's in your bank account right now. "How about $1200?" you say, and cringe inside. You know nothing about trucks or their value.

"What do you want it for?" Caroline says. "It's not exactly mint condition."

"Work," you say, which is more hopeful than factual, thinking of that job ad. "I need a truck."

"Are you a good worker?" Caroline asks.

It's at least half a lie, but you say, "Sure," because you somehow understand that a woman like this would not respect a man like you if you told the truth.

"Skip liked working," she says, looking past you to the driveway where the truck is parked. You look that way too. The fucking bird is back. "He mowed the lawn and he painted this house. Fixed what broke. Good with his hands and tools. Are you?" She looks at you again.

"Absolutely," you say, meeting her eyes. There are four tools in your toolbox in the hallway closet and you're counting a flashlight as a tool.

"You can have it for a thousand," she says. "It needs a tune-up and stalls if you go above fifty-five. And you'll need to clean out the cab."

You're surprised when she reaches out a crimped hand to shake on the deal, but you take it and it feels like worn cotton.

It is the first time you have touched anyone soft in months, and your eyes fill and you look away and say you'll come by later with cash and walk back to your house, flip flops slapping the driveway.

Then you call the number from the ad and talk to a man named Frank.

In a few days you'll become a landscaper.

§

Later that night you call Beth from the bar, because you want to give her the good news. You haven't had good news in a long time. She doesn't answer. You leave a message, going on so long that you get cut off, so you call back and leave another message, just to say goodnight.

§

On Monday you roll up to Frank's pole barn in the truck you haven't cleaned or tuned up yet, feeling lighter than you have in weeks. Like there are pebbles in your stomach instead of rocks. You get out and walk to where three men are standing. You introduce yourself and shake their hands, which are rough and hard and not like Caroline's at all. Then you don't know what to do, so you cross your arms with your fingers in your armpits and rock back on your heels.

"Sneakers aren't a good idea, bud," says Frankie, who is Frank's son. Frankie's tall and muscley but has eyes like a baby cow's. He's looking at your shoes. "Lose a toe that way. Gotta get you some good boots."

You glance at your feet and then theirs—all safe in leather and steel—and feel like a dumbass and nod and say you'll get some tonight. Then you wonder how you'd lose a toe. "How would I lose a toe?" you ask.

"Weedwhackers, chainsaws, scythes... you know," says Chad, the other guy. He's short and all his features are clumped together in the middle of his face.

"Oh, yeah," you say, and add a little "pssh" sound like you're not even that worried about losing toes anyway. At home your weedwhacker is electric and you have never touched a chainsaw, and what the fuck is a scythe.

"We'll put Greenie on the seed spreader today," says Frank, who looks more like a pudgy biker than the owner of a small landscaping business. "Chad, you're with Greenie. Frankie, with me. Load up."

You understand that you are Greenie and the nickname is a dickslap, but you nod and fake a smile. You hope you won't have to ask Chad how to work a seed spreader, that for once you'll be able to figure something out on your own.

§

You are driving home that night with the windows open to the cold wind, trying to blow out the musty smell lingering in the truck cab. Skip was a smoker. The ashtray is full, and you remind yourself to dump it out. Soon. But your freckly pale skin burned like forgotten toast today, even in half-ass spring sunshine, and it's making you shiver. You give up and hand-crank the window closed, then reach to do the same on the passenger side at a stoplight.

At this moment, a blend of smells fills the cab. Traces you didn't catch before. Cigarette smoke, sure, but also wood shavings and motor oil. Old Spice. Black coffee. You decide it's not unpleasant. You wonder what it would be like to smell that competent. Most days, you know, you smell like whiskey sweat.

When you pull into your driveway, you sit still for several minutes, hands on the leather-wrapped steering wheel, breathing deeply.

The porch light winks off next door and you go inside like that's what you were waiting for.

§

You are tired, so when you call Beth, you only leave a short message. "Hi Beth," you say. "I just got home from work. Coming home from work is less fun when you aren't here. I should have guessed it would feel like this."

§

It's Friday afternoon and you are sore and pissed off, helping Chad unload the truck that still feels like Skip's truck. You haven't cleaned it.

In your first week you got a sunburn on top of a sunburn. You haven't used your muscles like this in the decade since high school or maybe ever. You're plagued by hay fever. There is a patch of poison ivy on your left knee. Yesterday, you caught your right shin with a live weedwhacker string and it bled like rare prime rib. You bent a pushmower blade running over a tree root today and Frank said he's docking your pay to fix it.

Every night you've skipped the bar, because all you want to do is shower and fall into your bed. Frank wants trucks loaded and out by seven a.m., which means you have to be at his place by 6:30. This is the worst job you've ever had, and you are failing at it.

"I'm fucking spent," you say to Chad as you lift down a wheelbarrow together. "I don't know about this redneck, manual labor bullshit." You grab a half-full bag of Weed & Feed and plop it in the wheelbarrow, then try to wipe sweat from your face with your sweaty forearm.

Chad's smushed face puckers. "What's wrong with manual labor?" he asks. "You too good for it, college boy?" He hops into the truck bed to grab shovels and rakes closer to the cab, throwing them down at you instead of to you. A shovel handle catches you in the gut and it doubles you over.

You regret telling Chad about your community college certificate in Tourism & Hospitality. Straightening up, you say, "Asshole," through gritted teeth, then wish you didn't, because he hears you and jumps down.

"I'm not the asshole. You're the asshole, asshole. And maybe this job's too good for you," he says, then spits. It lands on the toe of your right boot. "You can barely push a fucking wheelbarrow, you tubby bitch."

You don't know if it's the shovel handle and the spit, or the sweat and the poison ivy, or the simple fact that you barely can push a fucking wheelbarrow, because more or less you are a tubby bitch, but you put your hands on Chad's shoulders and shove. He pings off the side of the truck and back at you, knocking into your chest like a medicine ball. You land on your ass in the gravel and dust.

"Fucker!" you say, and stop before adding, "No fair." You stand as Frankie jogs over, looking worried. His dad is in the barn checking returned items off the equipment list.

"Hey, bud," he says, glancing from you to Chad and back. "What's going on? Everything okay?"

"Greenie here says this job's beneath him," Chad says, crossing his arms. "He misses his loafers."

"I didn't!" you say. Not in those words. You do miss your loafers.

"And he shoved me," Chad says, uncrossing his arms. He takes a step toward you.

"He started it!" you say, then remember that actually you did.

"Enough," Frankie says, and Chad backs up. "Greenie?" Frankie's big dumb eyes are sad and you feel like a douche.

"I didn't mean it," you mumble. "Not like that." Your ears and cheeks flame, heating up your sunburn. Shit, are you going to cry? You turn to close the tailgate and when you face them again, Frankie's walking away and Chad is smirking.

You climb into the truck and start the engine and pull away, and it takes all your self-control not to jam on the gas and spray Chad with gravel.

§

A mile down the road, you stop gripping the steering wheel long enough to smack your palm against the dashboard. Fuck Chad. Why did he have to bring Frankie into it?

Frankie, who, you think, will probably tell his dad.

Frank will fire you this weekend, and all of it will be for nothing—the truck, the sixty-dollar boots, your battered body.

You tell yourself you're a moron, an idiot for thinking you could turn things around with a landscaping job, for believing you could make anything in your pointless life better.

You're thirsty for whiskey, and you deserve it after a week like yours. You have two twenties in your wallet and that will get you three doubles, four if you don't tip much.

Your throat aches, and you signal to turn right, toward Rookie's and your usual stool at the end of the bar.

But at this moment, a gruff voice in your head that isn't quite yours tells you to go home, that maybe you don't need the booze after all. That you could do with a shower and a meal and sleep instead, that things will seem better in the morning.

You blink and roll your window down, letting cool air flood the cab.

"Get a goddamn grip," you say out loud.

First you take life advice from a bird. Now you're hearing voices.

You just need a drink, you tell yourself.

You're thirsty and it's Friday.

You turn into the Rookie's parking lot and shut off the ignition.

§

At about half-past midnight, you pull into your driveway, parking the truck crooked. You sit, hands on the wheel, thinking of Beth. Of the look on her face as she drove away. A sob burbles up your throat and you clamp your lips shut, locking it in.

The porch light winks off next door and you go inside.

§

Before you fall asleep on the couch, fully clothed, boots on, you call Beth. It's one a.m. She doesn't answer.

"Fuck you," you say. When you can't think of anything to add, you hang up.

§

Saturday morning, you wake up with cottonmouth and a pounding head. Your belt buckle is digging into your stomach, and your shirt sticks to your back with sweat. You strip off yesterday's work clothes, throw them in a heap in your bedroom, and make a pot of coffee. You pull on a pair of pajama pants, stick your feet into flip flops, and swallow a few aspirins.

Shirtless, you head to the porch with a cup of coffee, up so early that you sit for an hour before Tim comes outside and turns on the hose.

"Nice farmer's tan!" he yells to you, smiling.

You look down, noticing the contrast between your pasty belly and red arms. The skin near your wrists is starting to itch and peel. Instead of answering Tim, you go inside to get a shirt and a refill. When you come back out, you see Caroline dragging a ladder from her garage. A bucket sits on the grass a few feet away, and that fucking cardinal swoops down to perch on the edge of it.

"Wait!" you shout, and it makes your head throb. You don't know what she's doing, but it looks dangerous, so you set your full coffee cup on the porch floor with a groan and jog over. The cut on your leg feels like it has its own pulse.

The cardinal flies away.

"Need to clean out the gutters," she says when you reach her. "Every spring Skip would do it. Spring and fall. How hard can it be?" She's wheezing from the ladder-dragging effort.

"Let me," you say, even though it's the last damn thing you want to do today.

Caroline doesn't put up a fight. "Suit yourself," she says. "But I'll hold the ladder. Then we can do yours." You groan on the inside. On the outside, you give her a tight-lipped smile.

The two of you get to work. Her twiggy arms don't look like they could do much to keep a ladder steady, but she holds on anyway, saying, "Be careful," every time you go back up to scrape another handful or two of wet leaves and muck into the bucket. You feel like dogshit and at first you fight both nausea and vertigo, but they subside and you work your way around her house, climbing up and down again and again.

You are almost done, when, on a trip down, your pant leg hitches on a loose screw and hikes up to your knee.

"Jesus H. Christ," Caroline says. "That's infected."

You're on solid ground now and you pull up the pant leg. The cut you got from the weedwhacker does look oozy and red. You poke at it with a dirty finger and Caroline slaps your hand away.

"Don't be a fool," she says. "You'll make it worse. Come inside."

You set down the bucket and follow Caroline in through the side door, across an over-furnished living room, down a hall, and into a pale blue bathroom. It smells like baby powder and there is shell-shaped soap in a dish on the sink.

"Sit," she says, pointing to the toilet. "Pull up that pant leg. Oof. You smell like the inside of a whiskey barrel." She takes a barrette from a drawer in the vanity and pins her hair back from her face. Then she washes her hands and gets to work.

That is when you learn that Caroline was a registered nurse for forty years, first at a grade school and then at a VA clinic. You also learn she is not gentle. She cleans your cut with a soapy washcloth in hard strokes, scraping off the pus-filled scab that formed and bringing tears to your eyes. The soap stings and when you draw in a sharp breath, she scolds you again.

"Think that hurts?" she asks. "Losing a leg would hurt worse. Infection's no joke. Buck up."

And you do, since she leaves you no other option. When she deems the cut clean, she slathers on something thick and antiseptic that also stings, then wraps your leg in a gauzy white bandage, securing it with medical tape.

"Tomorrow, we're going to do this again," she says.

You nod your head, tell her thank you, and follow her outside to finish her gutters and start on your own. She lets you use her ladder—"Skip's ladder," she calls it—and insists on holding it steady for you.

§

That night, sober and ashamed, you call Beth. She doesn't answer, but you stopped expecting her to long ago. You stopped even hoping she would.

"I'm sorry," you say. "I don't think I know how to not make things worse." You hang up.

§

Monday morning, you climb into the truck and start the engine with a pooling sense of dread. You haven't heard from Frank. You figure maybe the bastard just wants to fire you in person, wants Frankie and Chad to be there watching. You think about not going at all. Or beating Frank to it—quitting as soon as you see him. Either way, maybe he'll hand over your first and only paycheck, and then at least there'd be drinking money for the week.

About a mile down the road, your nose runs and threatens to drip. You arch your back to reach into your jeans pocket, but you must have forgotten your tissues at home. At a red light, you check the glove box. You find a wad of fast food napkins and a full carton of Senecas. You're not a smoker, but at this moment, you crave a cigarette more than you've ever craved a drink, and you rip open a pack.

Out of habit that isn't quite yours, you stick your hand in the crack of the bucket seat and pull out a Zippo, engraved with an "S" in swirling script. It lights with one flick.

The first drag makes you feel calmer, and by the time you're halfway to the filter, you wonder if last week wasn't so bad after all. Just beginner stuff. If you don't get fired, you can grab sunscreen and be less of a dumbass about poison ivy. Take some Benadryl. Be more careful with the weedwhacker.

§

When you arrive at Frank's, you tell Chad, "Morning," and try to mean it. Frankie walks over and looks at your feet, noticing that you're wearing your work boots. He smiles and slaps your back.

Frank grins. "Still with us, then, Greenie?" he says, thumbs in his belt loops. "Not sure you'd make it."

You nod.

"Where are your loafers?" asks Chad, trying to keep a straight face.

You peel a tab of sunburned skin from your forearm and flick it at him.

Frank guffaws.

You get to work.

§

You decide against calling Beth that night, but can't help texting her. "Work is going okay," you write, and hit send. Then you add, "I hope you are doing well."

She doesn't reply.

§

The next week, you pull into your driveway after work. It's mid-April and won't get dark until later, so you have to look hard at Caroline's porch to see when the light goes out. You know now that she waits up for you, though when you asked her about it a week ago, she seemed irritated.

§

"Do you think I can sleep and worry at the same time?" she said. "Not hardly. Not with my heart. Been waiting up for that truck longer than you've had hair on your chest. Just habit."

You smiled but held up your hands in surrender. "Just asking," you said.

"Well remember what curiosity did to the cat," she said. "And the groceries in the car aren't going to bring themselves in. Hurry up. There's ice cream."

You love ice cream, so you hurried, hoping she'd share.

She did.

§

When the light winks off, you stub out your cigarette and put your "Frank's Landscaping" hat on the passenger seat. You shut off the ignition and go inside.

You don't text Beth.

§

By early July, you've smoked eight packs of cigarettes. You tell yourself it's no big deal, since you only smoke three a day. One on the drive to work, one on the way home, and one in the driveway, while you wait for Caroline's porch light to go off. You skip weekends.

On Wednesday nights, you knock on Caroline's door so you can get her trash to put at the curb. On Sunday afternoons, you use Skip's riding lawnmower to cut Caroline's grass and then your own. Afterward, the two of you sit on her back deck and have a beer, but just one.

Sometimes after work you go out for sandwiches with Frankie and Chad. Yesterday, Chad picked up the bill. You were celebrating, because Frank asked you to stay on past the season. You'll trim and rake in the fall, plow and clear roofs in the winter.

"You're an okay worker, Greenie," Frank had said. Then he'd added, "I've had better. But you're okay."

You'd tried to play it cool, but failed, and your shit-eating grin embarrassed both of you.

§

You get home later than usual on a Thursday night in mid-July. You went for chicken wings at Rookie's with the guys after work, and orange hot sauce stains mingle with the grass stains on your white t-shirt. Your face and arms are so tan that it's hard to see your freckles.

You light a cigarette and leave the ignition on so you can hear the rest of the song playing on the radio. "All the Young Dudes" by Mott the Hoople leaks through the open windows and into the night, along with the smoke you exhale. It's dark and Caroline's front porch light is burning.

The final bars of the song play, but Caroline's light is still on. You shut off the radio and the ignition, and that's when you hear the two-part whistle of that stupid cardinal. Then you hear it again, and you feel a twist low in your gut. Something is wrong.

You hop out of the truck and jog to her door, knocking and calling her name. When she doesn't answer, you pound on it with your fist. Somewhere close by, the bird whistles.

You try the doorknob—it's unlocked. "I'm coming in!" you shout. "Caroline!"

The interior of the house is dim. The only light switched on is the one above the stove. In its weak glow, you see Caroline lying on the kitchen tiles, face down. Her right arm reaches forward, her left is pinned beneath her.

Panic hits at the same time you realize you left your cell phone in the truck. Your eyes dart around the kitchen. Caroline's old portable phone isn't in its cradle; it's not on the counter or the table. You kneel next to her, afraid to touch her. You put your ear to her back. She's breathing.

She mumbles something you can't make out.

"Hang on, Caroline," you say, then, "I'm sorry."

You turn her over and she moans. You check her head. It's not bleeding.

She mumbles again. This time, you understand. "It's you," she says.

You make a decision. "Caroline," you say, "we have to go. I need to pick you up. Hang on, okay?"

Tears blur your vision. You lift the tiny woman in your arms. She's easier to carry than a full sack of grass seed.

"Hang on," you say again.

Thirty seconds later, you're in your truck, Caroline slumped against you while you crank the ignition and jam on the gas. You reverse into the street and she falls forward. You hold her in place with your right arm, steer with your left hand.

You repeat, "Hang on hang on hang on," in a tight, high voice and you know you're begging. You feel her hand flutter and find yours.

At this moment, you are struck by a vision of a much younger Caroline—she is strong, laughing, blonde hair reflecting sunlight. She's wearing a halter top, jogging ahead of you, turning to call back, green eyes the color of spring grass…

"Caro," you say, but you never call her that. "It's not time."

She squeezes your hand.

§

You arrive at the hospital ten minutes later, carrying Caroline through the Emergency Room doors.

"Her heart," you tell a woman in blue scrubs at the intake station. "Please."

You rush to fill in the details of how you found her as an attendant brings a gurney.

You set Caroline on it. She's barely conscious but clings to your hand.

"It's okay," you tell her. "I'm going to be here. You go with them and I'll be right here." You know you're babbling. They wheel her away and you dig the heels of your hands into your eyes.

"We'll do everything we can," the woman says, her face kind. She writes something on a clipboard. "We'll set her up with oxygen, run some tests so we know what we're dealing with. But it may take a while. Are you family?"

"No," you say. "Well yes, kind of."

She waits for you to explain, and you do, about Caroline, about Skip—that now, it's pretty much just the two of you, how you're it.

You hope you're making sense, and you must be, because the woman nods and writes something else down.

"Alright," she says, gesturing to the waiting room. "You sit tight, and we'll let you know what we can. Or if you need to get home—"

"I'll stay," you say, louder than you mean to. "Sorry. I'll stay. I'm just going to have a smoke. I'm not leaving. I'll be right back. I'm not leaving."

You walk back outside through the double doors, sucking in deep breaths of cool air. You climb into your truck, open the glove box, and reach for a new pack of Senecas.

You smoke half of one before you break down, folding your arms over the steering wheel to hide your face while your shoulders heave.

Your phone rings from its place on the seat next to you, and you think at first that it must be the hospital, then remember they don't have your number. You wipe your nose on your shirt sleeve and look. Beth's name blinks across the screen.

You leave the phone where it is, unanswered, stub out your cigarette and open the door.

You need to get back inside.

You want to be there when Caroline wakes up.

FUNERAL HATS

Ginger owns a hat shop on the corner of Sixth and Moss. She sells many styles—bowlers, top hats, safari hats, derbies, jockeys' caps, fedoras, and berets. She does not sell baseball hats—they are bourgeois and hers is a shop of expensive hats.

Wealthy people look to Ginger's shop to meet the needs of their lifestyles—especially women. Women whose daughters are marrying doctors and dentists buy flowery pillbox hats. Women attending high-profile tennis matches buy wide-brimmed khaki hats to fashionably protect themselves from skin cancer.

Women spending weekends watching their husbands golf buy chic visors in pastel plaids and understated paisley prints. Women who are the mistresses of those golfers buy straw hats in fuchsia or teal to sip iced tea and vodka alone on their patios.

Of course, now that it is autumn, riding hats and fur-lined caps are more popular.

Then, of course, there are the funeral hats.

The funeral hats are exquisite.

Ginger believes that mourning should be done in style and with accessories. These hats are black, as funeral hats should be, with various trimmings: sequins, feathers, flowers, veils of black netting or lace.

Classy.

§

A woman looks over the funeral hats now, bending her trim waist to inspect a rhinestone buckle. Her blonde hair has just the right amount of gray at the temples—enough to say "experience" but not enough to say "done in." Her wrists are thin, one accentuated with a diamond watch, the other bare—less is more. Elegant calves in black silken stockings.

She is in her forties, or, if she's had work done, her fifties. She picks up one funeral hat, then another, turning them this way and that before setting them back down on the mahogany display table. Ginger walks over to her.

"May I help you select anything for your devastating occasion?" Ginger asks, being sure to speak in a tone of subtle sympathy. One wouldn't want to invite emotional displays, but coldness won't do, either.

The woman turns to face the shop owner. Ginger recognizes her. She came in a few months ago, was it February? She'd looked at the funeral hats then, too. In fact, she'd bought one. It was a lovely wool hat—if Ginger remembers correctly, it had been 1940s retro, with a braided band and black Swarovski crystals clustered on the side.

The poor woman, thinks Ginger. She's lost another loved one. Why must tragedy plague the beautiful?

"Yes, thank you," says the woman. "I'm looking for something, well, appropriate, with a short veil. I've just been widowed, and it's so, you know, *jejune* to show all of one's face at a funeral. Wouldn't you agree?"

"Of course," answers Ginger. "And I'm terribly sorry for your loss. I'm sure you're positively distraught."

"One always is with these kinds of things," replies the striking blonde as she picks up a particularly flashy hat, black silk with dyed ostrich feathers and a hand-made lace veil. She tries it on and looks at herself in a mirror.

"I think I'll take this one."

Ginger smiles sadly, head at a forty-five-degree angle, and wraps the woman's new funeral hat in tissue paper, placing it in a round hat box with wide ribbon handles.

"I can tell from your purchases that you have impeccable taste, ma'am." A compliment to turn the conversation away from the maudlin.

"Thank you," the woman answers. "The pieces here are beautiful, aren't they? Your shop is just the place for finding these…" she trails off, indicating her new hat.

"I do hope you'll come again," says Ginger as she hands back the woman's credit card. "Perhaps to shop for a happier occasion."

The woman looks like she would be a Derby regular, and would perhaps bring friends. Nothing like word-of-mouth marketing.

"My dear," says the woman, "the occasion is what one makes of it." She tucks her card back into her pocketbook.

"Remember that around every dark cloud there is a platinum lining. Until next time."

She smiles at Ginger and walks out of the shop, jingling the small golden bells above the door.

THICK ON THE WET CEMENT

hold it for you now.

looks heavy I would like to

In your hands your face

    I write them like that so when she's walking she can read them in the right order—the woman who makes my insides buzz.
    Her face never leaves the sidewalk directly in front of her, and I use colored chalk to make them stand out from the bleak cement and tossed-away gum wrappers.
    I saw her resting by the library like that two weeks ago, sitting on the narrow concrete retaining wall where the homeless people usually hang out. She didn't have an expression on her face as she stared at the ground and I hardly ever see her being still.

She's usually walking.

At first I mistook her for a man. She wears a baggy, gray ARMY shirt and black swishy track pants, her breasts loose and hanging just over her waistband. When it's hot she trades the pants for a pair of black spandex shorts.

Her stomach protrudes and I wonder if it's held babies that are grown now. Her cropped dark hair is sprinkled with silver and she is always alone.

A friend of mine, Bryan, said that one day he saw her stomping on a man as he lay on the sidewalk. She didn't say anything as she drove her sneaker down on his ribs. The man was curled into a ball on his side, whining like a small, frightened animal.

Bryan didn't know why she was so angry.

§

After weeks of seeing her do laps around Morgantown, I decided to say hello. *Don't do it,* Bryan told me over the telephone, reminding me of the man on the sidewalk. But he doesn't know that every time I see her a little thrill of electricity frizzles from my spine to my fingers; plus, I figure someone who is always alone might like to have a conversation now and then with another person. One who understands her, or tries to. Is trying to.

I usually pass her on High Street on my way to Jay's Daily Grind, the coffee shop I like, and that day, in a non-threatening beige blouse, I thought to myself, *Here I go.*

I inhaled as I saw her coming, feeling the usual thrill of her, and I smiled. I said *Hi.* She didn't look up and I thought maybe she didn't hear me.

So I said *Hi* again the next day, pausing for a moment in front of her for emphasis, like I really meant it. Not like the people who say *hi* just because your eyes meet theirs in line at the grocery store.

But I had to jump out of her way, because she didn't look up or seem to even notice I was there. I cut my knee on a fire hydrant when I did this, but though it stung and bled, I didn't say *Ouch* because I was busy staring at her as she walked away from me.

The scab is shaped like a mouth.

will chatter of you.

scar from the fire hydrant it

I hope I get a

I left that the next day right by the fire hydrant. I put it in pink chalk this time like the color my brand-new skin will be after the smile-shaped scab falls off. I hope she saw the words and thought of me, the girl who cared enough to get out of her way, to say hello twice without being told anything in reply. Something for nothing.

§

I live in a small efficiency up by the Ramada Inn, at the end of a long dead-end road. Nearby, there are nicer apartment complexes, but they're more expensive and I can't afford them.

The thin man who lives across the parking lot from me likes to sit outside in a folding chair. His name is Gary. I've told him lots of times that my name is Lara, but he always calls me *Young Lady*. I say *Good morning* to him and he tells me how the weather will be and what the leaves are about to do.

He told me two days ago that they're about to start falling, though I thought that was obvious, and then he described the first chapter of a novel he's writing about extraterrestrials.

He's working up to a large-scale battle scene in chapter ten, but told me not to worry because the humans win. I watched his hollow chest, how it heaved up and down in thin arcs as he spoke.

Aside from Gary and the mailwoman I wave to, my apartment complex is pretty lonely. It's full of retired people who stay indoors and people who often leave town for business. It has a motel feel to it, like no one is planning on staying long, like they don't even want anyone else to know they're there.

I get bored a lot. There's a window in my apartment, but the only thing to look out on is the parking lot, and in nice weather, Gary. I don't have cable. Sometimes, for something to do, I construct poems out of words I cut from the free Saturday paper. I choose interesting words like *October* and *Vascular* and put them in a red plastic colander. I shake them out onto the coffee table and read them how they fall.

§

    A few days a week, after work, I avoid going straight home to my empty apartment. I sit in the front window of Jay's on a high stool and I count how many times the walking woman passes—when she does, I feel that nice *zip-zap* in my body. One day I sat there for four hours and I counted seven times. At the coffee shop you can't just sit, so I bought four large cups of cappuccino and a raspberry scone. I left the window a few times to visit the ladies' room and I hope I didn't miss one of her laps.

    My friend Sheila and I used to meet for coffee on Saturdays, but since she got together with her girlfriend I don't see much of her. Last month, Bryan moved two hours away for a job in marketing. Aside from them, I have a few other friends, but they all have jobs or kids or spouses. They're busy. They tell me they don't have a lot of time to hang out, and I try to understand.

§

    The woman I watch doesn't wear any makeup. Her face is brown from the sun, which makes me think she doesn't wear sunblock, either. I wonder if she'll get skin cancer because she's outside so much. I'm concerned and tell her, because that's what friends do.

tricky mercury.

slowly like a mad hatter's

The sun's damage acts

    I write this poem in yellow chalk, the color of *Caution,* in front of the coffee shop very early on Saturday. I sit in the window so I can see her face as she reads it. At nine-oh-six she walks right over it and though I feel the tingle of her presence under my skin and smile, her face doesn't change at all. Her eyebrows don't raise and her mouth is still a line. I don't think she likes it. Maybe she doesn't understand it. As I sip my second cappuccino I imagine smearing a greasy line of white sunblock down the bridge of her sharp nose.

§

Today she's wearing a hat. It's beige with a gold and blue WVU stitched onto its front. Her face is scowling but safe, shaded by the protective brim. Looking at her gives me goosebumps, and I peer at the shallow crows' feet around her dark eyes and I know they won't get any deeper today. Her elfish ears are still left vulnerable, but I take the hat as a sign that she liked the poem after all, that she realizes someone cares for her, that she is special. I leave another one, to let her know how things could be, how we could spend our Sunday afternoons in the spring.

both of your eyes closed.

I'd like to read you a book

Under a shade tree

This is on Pleasant Street, written in green because I heard that color therapy is a thing and that green is calming. I imagine what it would be like if we were friends, if she gave me a chance. We'd run into each other on High Street near the dry cleaner's and I'd casually ask her if I could buy her a gelato. She'd be hot from exercising and say *Yes.* She might get something in a tropical flavor, like mango or pineapple or pomegranate. I would get vanilla and maybe she'd tease me for being boring. We'd sit on a bench and watch people as they went by. When she left me to go home, I'd say *I'll see you tomorrow* and she'd say *Yep,* just like that, because she'd know I was telling the truth.

§

I work at a car dealership by the river. We don't sell many cars, especially because gas prices are so high. No one is buying SUVs and half of our lot is full of them, shining in the sun as they decrease in value. I sit behind a small desk that overlooks the avenue and I watch people going by on bikes. I wave to them if they look at me.

My boss doesn't come in much because business is slow. There's no one for me to talk to, since I'm the only employee besides Veronica, who files things. She's forty-three and pregnant, and on bed rest. Her doctor said she's high risk and can't work. My boss said *Fine,* because that's one less person to pay—there's no such thing, he said, as paid maternity leave for part-timers.

Even though there's nothing to file, I miss Veronica. Without her, there's no one to have coffee with. I can never drink a whole pot by myself, so I pour the leftovers into a large fern in the front window. He seems to like it. His leaves are dark green and stretch toward the sun. I've named the fern Folger, and I address him when I say something out loud at work, like *Good morning* or *I couldn't sleep again last night.* I know Folger is only a plant, but it's better than thinking in silence all day. We don't have a T.V. there and I'm not supposed to make personal phone calls, though sometimes I do sneak a call to Bryan. I haven't told him about the poems.

I could do the same.

but he listens politely

Folger is quiet

This one was just a practical thought I had at work and I wrote it on Willey Street in front of the Methodist church. I printed it in white chalk since I knew the poem was stark and unlovely. I also knew the woman wouldn't know who Folger was, but thought she might get the point anyway.

After I wrote it I wandered down Willey Street and stopped in front of St. John's Catholic Church. The evenings are getting chilly and I shivered. Since I had nowhere to be I stood still and stared up at the church's windows. I wondered if I should commit myself to this parish or any parish—I was never baptized, so my choices are wide open. I thought about that—about why I haven't ever bothered with church, and I looked to my right when I heard approaching footsteps.

It was her. *Zip-zap,* all the way to my fingers. She wore the track pants and a fleece jacket. I shoved my chalky fingers deep into the pockets of my windbreaker and stepped forward to let her pass. I thought I heard her mutter *Thank you,* but I couldn't be sure.

The wind was picking up and college students swarmed the streets. As I looked at her receding figure, I realized I had expected her to walk in the other direction—that the poem would be upside down to her. I hoped she could figure out the way it was supposed to be. I almost called after her, to tell her to go the other way, but a group of four screeching girls passed in front of me and cut off my view.

I drove home. It was too cold for Gary to be out. I checked for mail but there was none. I called Bryan; he was busy. Same with Sheila. I got out my scrapbook of newspaper poems and read them out loud, but none of them meant anything to me. Lying on my fold-out couch, I looked out the window until the last bit of light was gone and I could see the silhouettes of my neighbors moving behind their window shades.

§

Today it's raining. My wool sweater is getting damp and I'm trying to hurry because I have to be at work in an hour and I still need to eat breakfast. The blue chalk writes thick on the wet cement and my words show up bold, standing out like they're on a blackboard in a classroom. I'm trying to write fast, but the rain is coming down harder and it runs into my eyes. I blink it away, wipe my forehead with my soggy sleeve.

it's chilly today.

cup of coffee or a scone

Let me buy you a

I'm shivering by the time it's finished and my blue piece of chalk is worn down to a nub. The poem is on the corner of Spruce and Willey. I get up from my crouch and jog in the direction of Jay's, squinting to keep out the water, trying not to slip in my slick-soled ballet flats.

I stop when I reach High Street. Cars are flying by, taking the corner too fast; maybe the drivers don't want to be out in this weather. I punch the crosswalk button and turn around, regretting that I didn't wear my raincoat.

I feel her before I see her, head down, t-shirt soaked, passing the BB&T. I freeze for a moment when I realize she's heading into the street just as a pickup is turning onto High from Willey.

Frantic, I slosh through a puddle and dash the three yards that separate us. I grab her, yell *Wait*. She whirls, fierce, looks from me to her blue-smudged shoulder, my fingers still clutching her sleeve. I don't let go because I don't want to.

She narrows her eyes—brown—for the first time, I'm close enough to see what color they are. I look meaningfully into them, tell her, *Hold on, I'm your friend*, but she doesn't hear me, or maybe she doesn't trust me.

She grabs my forearm so hard it hurts, pinches, her fingers like metal tongs, but for just a moment, there on the street corner, we're holding onto each other. Then she shoves me down to the wet sidewalk.

I land on my right hip and it hurts so much I almost cry. I lie there, stunned, rainwater pooling in my left ear. *I was trying to save you,* I yell after her, but she keeps walking.

§

I'm sitting in Jay's and I was supposed to be at the dealership twenty minutes ago. I'm on my second cup of hot tea and I'm not shivering as much anymore. The rain is coming down lighter now.

It's warm in here and the girl behind the counter said a batch of cranberry muffins will be ready soon. My sweater is dirty from the puddle and there's a tear in the elbow I hope I can patch. My forearm aches, and I can still feel where her fingers dug in.

She's walked by twice now and she must have seen it, the blue invitation on the sidewalk. If it hasn't washed away. If she hasn't changed her route.

The second time she passed she looked at me through the window—can she feel me, the way I feel her? That same tingle and rush?

Her chin tilted up and her damp forehead wrinkled, like she was thinking hard—about me, I hope. Either way, she didn't seem so angry anymore.

I'm waiting across from an empty chair, thinking next time, she'll stop in. She's got to be chilly by now, too.

SIX O'CLOCK HOUSE

 I'm supposed to be in the Veggie House checking Swiss chard for snails and fungus gnats, but instead I grab my pack of cigarettes and the portable phone. I look to see where Maureen is, then duck behind the barn and sit on a stack of wooden pallets. The boards groan and bend beneath my weight.

 I light a cigarette, take a deep drag, and exhale. My watch says it's after three, so I call home.

 Alaina answers on the third ring. "Hey, Mom," she says. "Do you want to talk to Grandma or something?"

 "No," I tell her. "I'm taking a smoke break and figured I'd call to see how your Monday was going. To talk about school. Or whatever." I take another drag.

 "It was okay."

 I see a black jumping spider on the pallet next to me and blow smoke at it. It scurries away. "Learn anything new?"

 "Not really."

"Well, was it a good day?" I tap ash into the moss by my feet.

"Mom, I'm kind of busy. Can I just talk to you later?"

"Sure, honey. Sure." I hang up the phone and stand. I smash my cigarette out in a clod of mud. Tonight I'll work late in the greenhouses.

§

"Remember," Gerri scolds me on Wednesday as she leaves the shop, "I want 'Coral Spice' geraniums, not 'Hot Rosy Blow' geraniums."

My lips stretch over my teeth. I want to break one of the sixteen-inch terracotta pots over her head.

When I took the job here I didn't know I'd have to deal with people like her—twiggy, pinched bitches in ironed khaki pants who watch me sweat and struggle to gather the plants they want. I even carry their marigolds and snapdragons out to their cars for them.

How do they get the flowers into the ground without getting dirty? I picture them wearing coveralls and rubber gloves. Surgical masks so they don't have to smell the dirt.

§

The Help Wanted ad had read:

"DEPENDABLE EMPLOYEE NEEDED FOR FLORAL AND GREENHOUSE WORK. WILL TRAIN. APPLY IN PERSON, M&R GREENHOUSES."

I saw it two and a half weeks after my divorce was finalized, and thought working with plants might be good for me. Peaceful. I pictured myself in a straw sunhat, watering a greenhouse full of happy-looking daisies.

I applied for the job.

§

The "M" stands for Maureen, the "R" for Ramon, her husband. During my interview, Maureen and I sat at a warped picnic table. Ramon watched from the other side of the barn, tanned arms crossed, leaning against a rack of coconut liners.

Maureen barely glanced at my application. She studied my face and then asked, "Are you a Christian?"

I hadn't been to church in years and thought she may have been kidding, but her thin mouth had frozen in a brittle smirk. I had a kid. I'd just moved back in with my parents.

My life was crap and I had $57 in my checking account. My heart sped up and a sour taste rose in my throat, but I made myself smile and nod.

Maureen locked her watery blue eyes onto mine and said, "You're hired."

I glanced over at Ramon, whose sun-wrinkled face was curved in a smile. He winked, and my heart slowed down.

Maureen took me on a tour of the property, and I started work that afternoon.

§

Every day during lunch break, Maureen tells me how Jesus has blessed her, her family, and their business, and how she must put faith first and other shit like that. I've made a game of it.

Every time she says "Jesus" I eat a Cheeto. When she says "praise" I take a sip from my can of Coke. If she says "Lord" more than twenty times during break, I get to eat the Snickers stashed in my purse.

Maureen moves like a defective machine, body parts jerking and twitching. She's in her sixties but looks younger, with a moony face and bottle blonde hair.

I don't know how she and Ramon got together—he is calm and deliberate, with skin the color and texture of tree bark. His stooped posture and ropey muscles make it impossible to guess his age. He could be sixty or eighty.

Ramon doesn't go to church with Maureen. He spends Sundays in the Six O'Clock House, cleaning tools at his work bench in the back or just sitting on his stool, enjoying the quiet.

The Six O'Clock House is my favorite of the greenhouses, too. It's just behind the shop, several yards to the right of the Second Geranium House. Inside, it feels kind of like a chapel, or maybe a cemetery. Private and peaceful and a little sacred, like nothing can touch me. And everything planted there grows.

§

I walk through the First Geranium House now. The black metal wagon I'm pulling behind me keeps getting stuck in the gravel and it's pissing me off. I'm collecting what I need for Gerri's order, being careful to double-check the smeared list in my sweatshirt pocket.

Last week I put the wrong geranium color into her chipped stone planter of annuals. She told me the petals clashed with the cushions of her patio furniture, and brought it back for me to fix. Because everything else in the planter already looked half-dead, it all got tossed and I have to redo the whole damn thing.

The cow can't even remember to water her plants.

I sneak a quick cigarette in the windbreak of the Second Geranium House, which is hidden directly behind the First. Maureen doesn't like me to smoke around her since she "quit for the Lord." She tells me I should take better care of the body "He" gave me. She also makes passive-aggressive comments about my weight. Bitch.

As much as Maureen irritates me, though, being here is better than being at home. Alaina, my twelve-year-old daughter, gives me more shit than Maureen and all the customers combined. I work late on purpose, offering to close so I can be alone with the plants. Their indifference is a relief.

I slip back into the First House and walk down the aisle between hundreds of geraniums in twelve different shades. I hate geraniums. Their spent petals don't shrivel and fall off. They shatter, leaving behind bare brown bloom heads on thin stems. They have to be broken off one by one. It takes hours of walking up and down the wide rows, snapping off the dead parts and dropping them into a plastic tub that I push along the gravel. I don't know why geraniums are so popular in graveyards. What a shitty tribute.

The "Coral Spice" geraniums ordered by Gerri are florescent orange-pink. They're garish, and only a shade pinker than the "Hot Rosy Blows." I wonder who the hell thought up their names—I feel like an asshole when I have to say them out loud. I load four pots into my wagon and add vinca vine, tall spike grass, and dusty miller. All the generic crap that middle-class people love. My planters at home are unexpected, full of fuzzy blue ageratum, pale yellow gerbera daisies, Blackie sweet potato vine, and lavender annual phlox.

I'm proud of them, but Maureen told me not to suggest that combination to shoppers. "They like what they like," she said. Which means that in my four years of working here, I've made hundreds of red-and-white-themed annual planters—tall spike grass in the middle, two red geraniums, two white geraniums, and two trailing vinca vines around the edges. Unless it's a smaller pot, and then it's one spike, two geraniums, and one vinca. Not that I really blame the plants. They don't aim for mediocrity, either.

I pull my loaded wagon all the way behind the Second House for another smoke. A full five-gallon bucket of blue liquid sits on the ground next to me, homemade fertilizer that Maureen mixes up, and I tap my ashes into it. A few feet away there's a bucket of green liquid—weed killer. I made up a rhyme so I don't mix them up:

I used blue and the plants grew; to kill them dead I put green in their beds.

I only get to the fourth puff of my cigarette when I see Ramon over by the back door of the Six O'Clock House. He's kneeling in the gravel, murmuring like he does, head down. Curiosity beats nicotine and I stub out my cigarette, leave my wagon, and get closer.

I try to step quietly but the gravel makes it impossible. Ramon hears me and looks over his shoulder, a sad smile crinkling the skin by his eyes. He turns toward me and I see he is holding one of the barn cats, the calico, her body folded in on itself, blood leaking from her mouth.

"Hit by a car," Ramon says, looking back down. "Dragged herself here." He pets the top of her head with his index finger. She wheezes.

"She's suffering," I say, feeling panicked and useless. "We need to—"

"Shhhh," he says. "This is all we can do sometimes. Just let 'em go." Then he turns his attention back to the cat, murmuring to her again.

Just let 'em go. I've heard him say that before. I've seen that same steady gaze. When last year's perennials didn't make it through the winter. When the ficus trees got root rot. Once, as he stood over a fallen bird's nest, black ants crawling on the gasping chicks still inside. Sometimes he looks at me like that, too, like he can see everything—the beginning and the end and what's folded up in between.

I feel like I'm intruding and I step away. I fetch my wagon and before I'm even back to the barn I hear the sound of a steel spade hitting gravel.

§

The next day, just outside the back door of the Six O'Clock House, I see a hump of freshly worked soil. A tiny climbing rose is the grave's only marker, one thin vine already reaching for the building's exposed framework.

§

Friday night, at home, Alaina rolls her eyes when I ask her about her week. My mother tells me there's leftover chicken in the fridge, but they didn't save me any sweet potatoes.

"She doesn't need those anyway," my father mutters, thinking I can't hear. I skip the chicken. My bed creaks when I climb into it. I let my stomach gnaw itself until I fall asleep.

§

As soon as I walk into the shop today, Maureen scolds me for over-watering the tomato plants. They're getting too leggy and not setting blossoms, she says.

I listen and nod, apologize, tell her I'll be more careful. But when I watered the plants yesterday they looked fine to me.

Ramon had been shuffling around somewhere in the back of the shop, but slipped away before Maureen tore into me. He can sense her moods before they hit, the way animals smell approaching storms.

It's Thursday, and she's been on my case for days. I think it's because on Tuesday she heard me say "Goddammit" when I sliced my finger open on a broken flowerpot. I apologized right afterward, but she's been snapping at me ever since.

When she's done bitching about the tomatoes, Maureen tells me I'll have to transplant nicotiana seedlings in the Six O'Clock House. She says it like it's a punishment.

I play along, looking disappointed, but smile when her back is turned.

§

Maureen has complained to me several times about how she hates this house. The Six O'Clock House is the oldest of all the greenhouses, here since forever, the property passed down through Ramon's family.

She says there's something wrong with the ventilation, that she can smell mildew in here. That the ground never really dries beneath the plant tables. She's told Ramon to move his workbench to another greenhouse or one of the dozen rooms in the barn; he won't.

Maureen's right about air in this house—it's wet and heavy, so damp that cigarettes won't light. But that's not the real reason she won't come in here.

It's called the Six O'Clock House because there used to be a clock hanging on the wall that stopped on six no matter how many times we changed the batteries and reset it. After more than a year of this, Maureen got spooked and threw it away. She said there's only one trickster, and she wouldn't give him a toehold on her property—something like that.

The plants in here grow twice as fast as the ones in the other houses. The flowers seem brighter, leaves glossier, stems thicker. Maureen won't admit that, though, and we just use the Six O'Clock House for new transplants and overflow orders.

§

It takes me a moment to notice that Ramon is standing at his worktable in the back, slowly turning the pages of a seed catalogue. It's the first time we've been alone since the day he held the dying barn cat. For some reason, I didn't want to mention it in front of Maureen.

"The rose, out back," I say. "That was nice."

He doesn't turn around. I think maybe he didn't hear me, but then he stops turning pages.

"She deserved a nice spot to rest," he says. "Everyone does."

Then he walks out the back door and leaves me to my work.

I refocus and turn to the middle plant table. It runs the length of the house, measuring about thirty feet long, three high, and six across. It's made of old chicken wire stretched over crude pieces of lumber. This is so excess water drips through the bottoms of the nursery pots to the greenhouse floor, keeping the plants' roots from rotting. The aisles are still clay and gravel, but after years of water falling beneath the tables, carrying little bits of soil and fertilizer, the ground there has become a lush tangle of weeds and tall grass. I dropped a small trowel in there once and never found it.

I've already covered the tables with rows of soil-filled transplant trays called flats, set up next to the plug trays, and I search my pockets until I find my steel transplant fork. It's actually for seafood, meant to pry crab meat out of the shell. But its two sharp prongs are great for jabbing holes into soil and for picking up seedlings by their stems.

With it I lift and transplant thirty-seven flats of nicotiana seedlings. After a few weeks of growing, their star-shaped flowers will bloom in warm-toned reds and yellows. I bought a pack of them with my employee discount a few days ago, but haven't got around to planting them yet.

§

It's Friday and Alaina has early release from school because of some kind of teacher training. I'm going to surprise her by picking her up—Maureen is letting me duck out early since I agreed to cover Sunday alone. Usually Alaina rides the bus or walks with friends, but I want to take her for ice cream.

Yesterday, I noticed a Social Studies test on the fridge that she got a 95 on. Maybe if I take her to celebrate, she'll tell me more about school, or anything. So often, she feels like a stranger to me.

At half-past three I pull up near the front door of the middle school in my '09 Taurus. Its blue exterior is a little rusted, but it runs well. Aside from Alaina, it's the only thing I got from the divorce.

The sky looms dark but I hope the rain will hold off. The ice cream place only has outdoor seating. I don't see Alaina in the crowd of kids standing around waiting for rides, so I turn off the engine and get out, dropping my cigarette onto the pavement.

I head toward the door, weaving around teenagers and discarded bookbags. I see my daughter, a few yards to my right, standing with three girls I don't know. I wave. She doesn't wave back, but maybe she doesn't see me.

I bend over to tie a shoelace that's come loose on my Keds, but leaning down makes me cough. While I'm still trying to clear my throat, I hear one of Alaina's friends ask her, "Who's that lady?"

Expecting an introduction, I straighten up and open my mouth to call hello. But Alaina hesitates, then shrugs. Her eyes meet mine and slide away.

I stare at her, not understanding for a moment. When I do, there's no air in my lungs. The ground tilts but I make it back to my car. As I pull away, the first fat raindrops splash against the windshield.

§

That night in bed, I lie awake, sweating into twisted sheets. Alaina's rejection shouldn't be so shocking. It's just another moment in a long line of humiliation and hurt, but alone in my room, the scar tissue is ripped away and I'm left raw and stinging, reliving those times I've felt like less than nothing.

In seventh grade, I was so proud of my school photos. I'd worn my favorite teal sweater dress and pink lip gloss for picture day, and spent an hour that morning curling my hair. I thought I looked like Alyssa Milano.

When the photos came in I waited for my dad to make a geeky joke about chasing boys away. Instead, he studied them for a minute, then laughed and said, "Well now, who are you trying to be?"

My mother said nothing. I threw away the picture order form every year after that.

In eleventh grade, I got my first real crush on a boy and tried to give myself a new image. I bought tight jeans, wore tons of black mascara, and fixed my hair in a high ponytail every day.

In the mirror over my dresser, I'd practice sexy looks. At a basketball game one Friday night, I sat near some girls I knew a few rows in front of my crush. Between quarters, I got up the nerve to turn around and make eye contact.

I flipped my bangs off my forehead, pouted my cherry-colored lips, and even gave him a flirty little fingertip wave. He nudged a boy next to him and pointed at me.

They both laughed, but I didn't know they were being cruel until they started making cow noises. I left the basketball game and walked home alone.

When I got engaged, I tried again. I went on a diet. I got a new haircut, waxed my eyebrows, shopped at JCPenney instead of Kmart. And for a little while it worked. Until it didn't. By then, though, I had Alaina.

But I don't anymore. I haven't for a long time.

I turn to my side and dry heave into my pillow, pressing my face down hard so that no one will hear me.

§

Saturday's shift feels endless—sounds delayed, images out of focus. After too many botched register transactions, Maureen tells me to water shrubs in the cold frame and pull myself together. When I get home I go straight to bed, not bothering to change my clothes. But the night creeps by with no sleep to help me waste the hours.

§

Sunday morning, Maureen is hurrying, gathering wire, silk flowers, and small fake birds for her monthly senior citizens' craft project. She's going to the old folks' home right after church.

She spits instructions over her shoulder, something about someone's planter and a shipment of geraniums that need to be pulled, but I don't really hear her. She doesn't wait for me to respond, and a moment later, her tan SUV pulls out of the empty parking lot.

Ramon won't be in today either, and that works for me. Maureen mentioned on Friday that he'd be out picking up a load of peat from the wholesaler two counties over.

The morning passes quietly—a few customers in for annuals, one guy buying shrubs, another fertilizer. I'm calm and efficient, moving through the shop and barn, making my own arrangements between customers.

From the trunk of my car, I get the six-pack of Slim-Quik I bought weeks ago. I also grab the packet of nicotiana seeds I never got around to planting. I put them both in the wagon I've pulled behind the counter and wait on another customer.

Then I put my car away, driving it into the back of the barn, parking behind Ramon's broken-down tractor. No one comes back here, and the dirt floor is so hard packed that I don't leave tire marks or footprints. I check the clock. It's just past one.

Maureen keeps extra plant chemicals on a shelf in the bathroom, and from there I take an eight-ounce jug of GroMate—a fertilizer that comes in pellet form. Each pellet is about the size of a baby aspirin.

Before I leave the bathroom I toss my pack of cigarettes in the garbage. I add the GroMate to my wagon and check my sweatshirt pockets until I find my transplant fork. I'll need it later.

Against the back wall of the shop we keep gardening tools and seasonal bulbs that didn't sell earlier this spring. Bulbs can be forced in the right conditions any time of the year.

From there I pick out a child-sized steel shovel, a small bag of lime, and a variety of bulbs: purple and white hyacinths, yellow and orange tulips, and several varieties of crocus. Next I go to a spinning rack of seeds, grabbing blue morning glories and pink sweet peas. I dump it all into the wagon with the rest.

I look again at the clock. Not quite three. I have time for a break, so I fish my last candy bar out of my purse. It's a king-sized Snickers, and I savor every bite, grinding the peanuts to a paste and sucking the chocolate from my teeth.

§

I'm supposed to keep the shop open until four, but at 3:30 with no customers, I think it's close enough. I lock the front door and flip the sign to "Closed."

I shut off the phone's ringer and turn the answering machine on.

I leave through the side door and walk to the First Geranium House, threading between the plant tables to where the irrigation system is set up. Ramon built it last year especially for this greenhouse, because this one holds the most flowers. His invention is made up of a thick main hose connected to a spigot, with thinner hoses branching off of it.

These smaller hoses are full of tiny pinholes, and are laid on top of the geranium pots, between the soil and the foliage. When the water is turned on, all the pots are slowly flooded. It takes about two hours.

There's also a pumping system hooked up to the spigot, so that fertilizer can be added directly to the water.

Just outside the back door of the greenhouse I find what I need next: a bucket of green liquid. I carry this inside, careful not to spill any. I put the bucket down next to the pump, add a siphoning hose, and flip the power switch. I set the pump's timer for two hours and turn on the tap. The main hose plumps, but I don't head back to the shop until I hear the quiet flush of water filling the drip hoses.

§

Inside the shop, my eyes fall on one of my recent floral displays. Pots of African violets fill a little wicker wheelbarrow, purple ribbon tied around one of the handles. I feel a pang of conscience, and decide to leave Maureen a quick note.

I'm sorry, I write. *I should have given a two-week notice.* I tuck it under the stapler without signing it.

That done, I pull my collection outside, shutting and locking the side door behind me. I add a small perennial clematis to my wagon and head to the Six O'Clock House.

§

Once inside, I spend a few minutes just breathing, like I do every time I walk in here. Then I grab my shovel, crawl deep underneath the wide middle plant table, and slowly, carefully, I dig.

§

By the time I'm finished, I'm drenched in sweat and covered in a layer of heavy black soil. All the better. I look at my watch—it's already after five.

The hole I've dug is about three feet by six feet, and goes two feet down, into the clay underlayer—I test it to make sure it's big enough. A few pieces of sharp gravel in the clay have to be picked out, but most of it is so small that it feels like sand.

I crawl out, making sure I don't tear the long blades of grass that hide what I've done. I make several trips back and forth like this, bringing in all my supplies from the wagon.

Then I push it outside through the double doors and close myself in, finding a cast-off metal fence post to fit through the handles. I hide my little shovel behind Ramon's workbench.

Ducking low, I crawl back in to settle my rear end into the soft dirt cradle. I pull off my sneakers and socks, open the first warm can of Slim-Quik, and use it to chase back half the packet of Nicotiana seedlings. They're tiny and it's easy.

I scatter the rest in the dirt around me. Next I swallow the crocus bulbs. They're the size of gumdrops and have sharp edges. They hurt my throat and I gag a few times, but not hard enough to quit.

Next I take my transplant fork out of my pocket, and with it I make a series of shallow cuts on my left forearm, cringing at the sting. I open the packet of sweet pea seeds and press each one into my skin.

The pain is almost too much and my eyes well, but I force myself to think of how good they smell when they're in bloom. Tiny trickles of blood drip onto the ground at my side, the red disappearing into the soil's blackness.

After a few minutes I repeat the process on my right arm, this time pushing morning glory seeds into the cuts. Since the hyacinth and tulip bulbs are too big to swallow, I bury them underneath my outstretched legs.

Then I cover my legs with a layer of dirt. It feels luscious and cool when I wiggle my toes in it, reminding me of the trips Alaina and I took to the beach when she was little. I frown and force away the memories. Focus on what I'm doing.

I sprinkle the lime on top and all around me, coughing when some of it floats into the air. I fold the emptied paper bag up and shove that into the soil, too.

I work the clematis out of its pot—it hasn't bloomed yet, and its tag was lost in last month's windstorm—so I don't know what color its flowers will be.

I gently pry apart its root base until the whole plant is flat enough to wedge comfortably beneath my head when I lie down. This takes a few tries, but finally I get it to curve around my neck like an airplane pillow.

The last part is the hardest.

I have four cans of Slim-Quik left. My watch says ten to six. I sit up, open the jug of GroMate, and swallow a few pellets at a time. The chalkiness of the Slim-Quik covers up a lot of the chemical taste, but I still have to concentrate hard not to throw up.

My stomach cramps and about halfway through the bottle I have to stop. I can't swallow any more. I hope it's enough.

I toss the bottle down next to me and let my body drop back, head cushioned by soil and clematis roots. I sweep dirt over myself, wrapping up in a blanket of loose earth. The cuts on my arms clot with mud and stop bleeding.

Time passes—hours or minutes. Just as my thoughts drift and blur, the sound of the back door opening cuts through the fog. A slow step, the creak of Ramon's body settling onto his stool.

No.

How could I forget to lock the back door?

I want to protest. I've worked so hard. I'm whimpering, but maybe not out loud.

Then a low humming starts up in the back of my brain, a slideshow of images flashing—my daughter's blank face, the dying cat, my father laughing, transplant trays, my daughter's face, the dying cat, my daughter, my daughter.

The humming gets louder, or maybe it's the whimpering. Something rises in pitch, hurting my ears.

Then, "Shhhh," I hear. "Shhh."

And all the noise stops, like sinking underwater. I can let go.

A new picture replaces the others. A movie, in slow motion. Me. The sweet peas and morning glories, both climbers, wrapping their arms around my own, weaving their clinging fingers between the bones of my wrists. The tulips and hyacinths pushing up through my thighs toward the light and the damp air.

The purple and white crocuses mixing with red and yellow nicotiana blooms, whorls of color where my stomach was.

The clematis coiling around my collarbone and shoulder blades, using them as a trellis to reach up through the wire of the plant table.

It's me, pretty.

Me.

DANGER: NO SWIMMING, NO FISHING

Sam had taken two wrong turns, driven down two country roads past corn fields and grape vineyards and forests and more *nothing* surrounding this hick-shit town Glenn had left her in, but cresting a long hill, she finally saw it: Hanover's old reservoir, shining below in the afternoon sun like a mirror just polished.

She coasted toward it and pulled her rusting Chevy to the side of the gravel road, two tires crushing knee-high weeds and purple wildflowers she couldn't name.

Leaving her keys in the ignition and grumbling about ticks, she tied her long brown braid into a low knot at the back of her neck, grabbed her camera, and climbed out to get the photos her editor wanted.

She regretted wearing sandals. To get closer to the water, she'd have to go down a slick berm of long, wet grass.

She knew she'd fall before she did, sliding on her hip and thigh, staining her long skirt and tearing the elbow of her denim jacket. She thanked her bad luck for not being worse; the camera wasn't damaged. If she broke it, the cost to replace it would come out of her already small paycheck.

Swearing at herself and nature, Sam got to her feet, finding herself just inches from where the water lapped the shore in slow, gentle caresses.

Her next curse died in her throat.

She held her breath.

Cicadas buzzed in the air around her. A hawk screamed and wheeled above. Her eyes locked onto the water's surface; she stared, entranced by the sunlight playing over the ripples.

The cicadas got louder. The hawk screamed again and again...

Sunlight on ripples.

Buzzing cicadas.

A screaming hawk.

Sunlight on ripples.

Buzzing cicadas.

A screaming—

Then a different sound broke in: dim at first, the way an alarm disrupts a dream. Confusion shifted to fear before she came back to herself, realizing the sound came from her phone—that it rang from somewhere behind her, its shrillness muffled. Why didn't she have her phone? And something else was wrong—

She gasped and looked down to see she stood shin-deep in cold water, her bare toes sinking in silt, the hem of her skirt soaking, the chill setting into her bones.

Then the phone again, incessant.

She whipped her head toward the bank; it stretched six long feet behind her. And farther away, her sandals, lying where she must have kicked them off. But she didn't remember doing that—didn't remember wading in, either, and why would she have, anyway? New skirt and bare feet in cold, dirty water when all she needed was a photo or two.

She turned back, looking out across the water, trying to remember.

A cloud passed over the sun. With the light's reflection gone, she could see just beneath the surface. She squinted and leaned down—something was there, just in front of her. Something small and pale...

She took another step into deeper water, disturbing the silt and sending up a dark cloud. The water lapped against her knees, and she waited for it to clear. Careful to stand still, she leaned closer.

Small, pale and—

Two dark eyes opened.

A face.

She screamed and splashed back to dry land, stumbling and catching herself, wet to the shoulder, sucking in panicked gulps of air. She felt too aware, suddenly, of just how alone she was at the reservoir.

She grabbed her shoes and phone and scrambled up the small hill, only then remembering she hadn't taken any pictures. She snapped two over her shoulder that would likely be blurred.

Then, ignoring the high grass and her fear of ticks, ignoring the pain of sharp rocks she stepped on, still barefoot, she ran for the sanctuary of her car, hurling herself inside and locking the doors.

Against what, she didn't know.

She gripped the steering wheel and tried to slow her breathing, which hitched in her chest like a skipping vinyl record.

After a moment, she looked at her phone: a missed call from Al, her editor. A text too: *Where are you?!*

The time read 4:47. She'd gotten there shortly after four. Where had almost an *hour* gone?

Sam dropped her phone in her lap. Closed her eyes.

It couldn't have been what she thought—the thing in the water.

She'd zoned out, she reasoned. Fine. No big deal—she was probably dehydrated. It had been a problem lately. Had she drunk anything but a cup of coffee that morning? Had she eaten any lunch? No.

And in the water—the face. It had to have been a fish. A carp, maybe? They got big, didn't they? Yes. Big as toddlers. And fish had eyes. (Could they close them? Could they open them? Could they look at a person like they needed something?)

She picked up her phone again, noticing how her hands shook. She texted Al, fixing typos before she hit send: *On my way.*

Then she took one last deep breath, put her sandals on her sore feet, and turned the ignition. Before pulling away, she noticed a peeling wooden sign, half-covered by wild raspberry canes: **DANGER: No Swimming, No Fishing.**

She raised her camera, focused the lens, and pressed the button.

§

Al had gone by the time she got back to the office. At the vending machines, she got a bag of potato chips and a bottle of water—better than nothing—and went back to her cluttered desk. She needed to finish the story that was already late: **Hanover considers selling defunct reservoir.**

In a town this small it was big news—not because half the residents even remembered there was an old reservoir, but because the offer was for $10 million, from some Buffalo billionaire who wanted to build a private hunting estate in the middle of what had become pristine wilderness.

From public records, Sam knew the reservoir hadn't been in use since the 1980s; the town had joined the county water district then, so it was abandoned, left for nature to do what it always does: reclaim.

She was supposed to get pictures of the ruined pumphouse, the caved-in causeway, and the twisting trees that grew unchecked right up to the water's edge.

But her only usable photo was of the sign.

She wrote a cutline, scanned her copy for errors, and dropped it all in the editor's queue.

§

That night, Sam dreamed of eyes underwater, a world gone liquid, a pull she couldn't resist. She woke in a sweat, fists gripping the sheets, and for the first time in weeks, missed Glenn.

It was just a dream.

It was just a fish.

Just a long day made longer by an hour strangely, inexplicably, gone.

§

"HOO-boy! Did you see those comments?!" Al called when she got to the office in the morning. "People are FIRED UP about your article!"

Sam rolled her eyes for show but smiled while she walked to her desk—comments fights were some of the only entertainment they got at the little newspaper.

She logged onto her computer and opened up the newspaper's social media. There they were: 167 comments.

Al appeared behind her.

"See?" he said, still delighted.

"The tree-huggers are pissed—they say there's eagle and owl nests there, that some of the trees are a hundred years old. Others, though, especially the redevelopment nutjobs, they say the town should sell, use the money to fix up the downtown, draw in some new businesses—chain stores, crap like that."

Sam scanned and scrolled as Al talked. She read comments full of cursing and conspiracy theories. Lots of name-calling. Words like "communist" and "Antifa" and "woke agenda" peppered the screen. Some of the nastiness sounded like threats.

"Did you block anybody?" she asked.

"Nah," said Al. "Controversy sells papers!"

"Not enough of them," she said.

They'd had to lay off the entire art department the month before, and the circulation "department" was down to just one person. Sam was one of two reporters, and Al covered as much as he could himself.

He loosened his tie that was already loose. A nervous habit, Sam knew.

"Yeah," he said. "I know. But seriously, do a follow up. Do a whole series. Keep on top of this one."

She swallowed.

That meant she'd have to go back.

§

It came to her at odd moments—that strange spell, the water, the face—in the days after. A feeling of wrongness when she thought of someone building a McMansion or a glamping-style hunting lodge on the reservoir. Or did that feeling come from the body of water itself?

Danger: No Swimming, No Fishing.

There on the sign, clear as day.

A place people shouldn't go.

Yet that's where she found herself after leaving the grocery store that weekend, except that it wasn't on the way home at all, and she told herself she must have wanted to take the scenic route, because there she sat, engine ticking over, staring at that sign.

Danger: No Swimming, No Fishing.

She tore her eyes away, started her car, and drove off.

§

Sam learned nothing new during public comments at the next Hanover town board meeting. Heading out of the building, though, she heard a woman behind her say "…let sleeping dogs lie. Ever since that poor thing drowned…"

Sam whirled around like she'd been pinched, searching for who said it, but the crowd jostled her and she had to catch herself on a dirty cigarette butt bin to keep from falling. She straightened up and looked, but the woman was gone.

She went back to the office.

§

At her desk the next afternoon, Sam called Fred Black, Hanover town board member and retired sheriff's sergeant.

She'd run into a brick wall at the office—none of the articles before 2005 were digitized, so she couldn't find anything on a drowning at the reservoir. But she knew if anyone living would remember it, Fred would.

Plus, he was chatty. A reporter's best friend.

After they had said hello, she got right to it: "Fred, what can you tell me about someone drowning in the old reservoir? Were you with the department then?"

She heard him suck in air, almost a whistle, then huff it out. She clamped the bulky landline receiver between her chin and shoulder, then readied her hands over her keyboard.

"A drowning… yes. Yeah, I do. Bad luck, that was," he said.

He paused again, and Sam could almost hear him cranking the memory up from whatever rusty place he stored it in.

"I wasn't supposed to be on—got brought in to help search. Late in the afternoon—I recall thinking I shouldn't have coffee, that it would keep me up, but I did it anyway, dammit. And I was right. Part of that was the trouble itself, though—seeing it, I mean. Up close. Part of the job, but… Not conducive to a restful sleep, that's for sure."

She still hadn't typed anything. "Fred?"

"Oh! Of course, of course. Anyway, the divers couldn't *find* him—can you imagine? Damnedest thing. Where could he have gone?" Sam's fingers skittered over her keyboard like busy spiders. "Then the kid surfaced, bobbed up like a buoy, and got caught against the causeway."

Her hands stilled. "Kid? Oh no…"

"Yeah," said Fred. "Kid. They were fishing. Wasn't posted back then—folks swam or fished sometimes, and the town didn't fuss. After that, though. Well. They had to."

"What happened?" she asked, typing again, catching up her notes.

"This is what we got: that day, father and son went out in a little canoe. Flimsy as shit, and no lifejackets. They were from Buffalo—city folks, at least to us. Daytrippers, assuming still water was safe water. *Never* assume that, young lady! Hear me?"

Sam promised him she did, shuddering at the memory of that pale, ripple-warped face.

"Even so, they shoulda known better," Fred said, quieter now. "The kid fell overboard—you know how kids are, you can't trust 'em to act right—and his dad went in after him. When they didn't come home, the wife called us. A unit went down and found the canoe flipped, the dad frantic. No kid. Sad day."

For a moment, neither of them spoke. Sam typed. But her neck ached, so she stopped to hold the receiver.

"That's… horrible," she said finally, sitting back in her creaking office chair. She stared at the water stains on the ceiling tiles. "But the father, he survived?"

"He did, at least for a time," Fred said. "There was talk of charging him—the father. But he was already broken, so what would be the point? Losing a child… Lord. That's its own punishment, and the guy ate his gun a few months later, anyway."

"Jesus," Sam said, but her mind was on Glenn now—how *he'd* mourned, and how he'd blamed, and how he'd left. Guilt flared in her stomach—not because it was her fault, but because she'd been *relieved*, and he could tell.

Fred was still talking, and Sam sat up straight, tried to pay attention. "...and well, after that the town kept folks out, and a year or two later we joined the water district, so that was that."

"That was that," she echoed. Hadn't Glenn said something similar? When he'd told her he would stay if she asked—if she begged. If she apologized. And when she didn't: *I guess that's that, then.*

And it was.

"I think that's everything I can tell you," Fred said. "Unless you have questions about something else?" He sounded hopeful.

"No—I mean yes. The father and son. Do you remember their names?"

"Sorry," Fred said. "Their faces, I do. But names, no. That was forty-odd years ago."

Sam said she understood, thanked him, and hung up.

§

When Al came in and she told him what Fred said, he advised her to "hit the filing cabinets."

She slumped. Before articles were saved digitally, they got clipped, by hand, and "filed." Except there were eleven filing cabinets, and no actual system—people put articles where they thought they should go.

"Try R for 'reservoir,' B for 'boating accident,' F for 'fishing accident,' and D for 'drowning,'" said Al, smiling. Sam hated the filing cabinets. Everyone did. "Good luck!"

"A friend would help, you know," she muttered as she walked away.

He heard her. "Lucky for me I'm just your boss!" he said, laughing. She heard his office door shut.

It took her over an hour.

She ended up finding it under W, for "water," she figured. Two paragraphs, short and somber.

Their names were Tom and Bradley Griffin.

Bradley was only seven.

He died August 26, 1986.

§

That dream again. Sam in the water—this time clutching wet newsprint that disintegrated in her fists. A fish the size of a Labrador loomed close, its big dead eyes morphing into the empty sockets of a human skull. When she tried to kick away, it bit at her toes.

She woke up, the sounds of its clacking teeth still sharp in her ears.

§

Al sent her back to the reservoir for decent pictures, like she knew he would.

She told herself to be rational. She ate before she went, drank plenty of water, wore sneakers and shorts. On the slick little hill, she side stepped, moving carefully.

No more wooziness. No more falls.

Get the pictures and leave, she told herself. *Five minutes, tops.* The camera's weight around her neck felt reassuring. Grounding.

Like before, an oppressive calm hung over the place. Sam stood on the bank, focused the camera lens, and took shot after shot of the still water. She zoomed in on the sunken causeway, grabbed by an impulse to find her way to it, walk along it as far as she could.

And if she should fall…

No.

She closed her eyes, and without wanting to, pictured a scared little boy thrashing underwater; a man screaming; a small body caught up like driftwood; police sirens; an overturned canoe. Questions no one could answer pinged around her brain like fireflies in a jar: *What was he doing when he fell in? Did he scream for his father? Or couldn't he do even that? How fast had he sunk that his dad couldn't get to him?* Then Fred's warning: *Never assume still water is safe water.*

She opened her eyes.

Fred was right. Plus, she'd promised him. No assumptions about still water. But the water in the reservoir wasn't still, not really. A soft breeze rippled the surface, creating a gentle current, sunlight winking on the ridges.

She watched it, lulled by its small, steady movements.

Don't, said that little voice of reason in her brain. The one that wanted to keep her safe. The one that said *Shhh* when Glenn had said *Beg me, Sam, beg me to stay…*

But the sunshine and the water called too: sparkling ripples, rhythmic little pulses, inviting her closer.

Get away.

But it was so beautiful. So soothing. And the past four months had been hard—too hard. Lonely and ugly and long.

No.

Sunshine on the water. Cicadas buzzing, like static in the background. A hawk screaming from its place in the sky. Heavy shoes; cold around her ankles, then her knees. Cicadas buzzing. The water rising higher. A hawk screaming. Sunshine on the water. She felt an urge to lie down; to surrender to fatigue, not unpleasant. A gentle current. Sunshine. Cicadas.

That voice faded away. Everything did.

Her body felt heavy, then weightless.

The sun shone above her. Bubbles floated up and away. A small hand gripped her own.

So small, cold too, and thin—pressing, clamping.

Then, it pulled.

No, the voice surged back. *No!*

Sam thrashed. She was underwater, and next to her, clouded by stirred silt that stung her eyes, that face. But not just a face—a body, gray-white, so pale, floating beside her. Arms like sticks, and a hand that wouldn't let go.

Dead eyes. All black.

Sam looked into them, stopped fighting as a shushing, liquid heartbeat pulsed in her ears, blocking everything else. Like the ultrasound she never got to hear. Hadn't wanted to hear.

The little hand gripped tighter.

Had it been her fault, after all? A wish that came true? She'd wanted it gone…

The face loomed closer. Her lungs burned.

No, the voice broke in.

No to guilt. No to babies. No to Glenn and no to whatever the fuck clutched at her, wanting her to drown, wanting her to *stay*.

She pulled her knees to her chest, and then, aiming for that gray-white face, she kicked with everything she had.

Her right foot connected, sinking into the thing's soft cheek. It let go and Sam broke the surface, coughing, gulping air.

She was exhausted, and her feet in their sodden sneakers felt like lead weights, but fear and something else drove her—anger, maybe, and she pulled herself toward the shore until her knees hit silt and then she clawed her way out, retching on the sandy grass, shuddering at the memory of that small, desperate hand.

She blinked water from her eyes and looked around her. The camera was gone—likely lost to the water, and ruined even if she was willing to go back in to find it.

She wasn't.

But her keys and phone lay nearby—she didn't remember dropping them—and she grabbed them, woozy with relief. Stopping only to slip off her soaked shoes and tuck them under her arm, she hurried up the small hill in a half crouch, still coughing.

By the time she dropped into the driver's seat of her car and fumbled the keys into the ignition, tears blurred her vision. She wiped at her cheeks with the back of her hand and took a deep breath, grateful that she still could.

She considered calling Al then, or the police, or maybe even Fred. But they'd all tell her to stay there, to wait for help. And she couldn't explain *why* she'd almost drowned. If she tried, no one would believe her.

She looked up. *Danger: No Swimming, No Fishing.*

"No shit," she mumbled.

She turned the ignition, put the car into gear, and hit the gas, spraying gravel.

In the rearview mirror, she watched as the sign got smaller and smaller, and then disappeared.

INHERITANCE

The will isn't complicated; he's an only child. Everything that was his mother's is now Ty's. The contents of her condo in Albany, a few grand in savings, her car, and his grandparents' farm.

§

Two days after he speaks to the lawyer, Ty is sitting with his grandmother at Twilight Meadow, the nursing home in Albany where she's lived for almost fifteen years. In that time he's visited twice.

"I'm sorry I haven't come to see you in a while," Ty says, scratching his chin. He doesn't really know what to say, though thankfully the staff already told her about his mom.

"Shep, honey, I know you're busy," she says. "And it's hard to get out of the city."

"I don't go by that, Grandma. Not anymore. Remember?"

His full name is Shepherd Tyler Coleman, after his grandfather who died the week before Ty was born. In college he dropped his hick name and introduced himself as Ty. He wanted something cool, something fitting for a financial analyst. He liked shaking clients' hands, two pumps and "Call me Ty." But the job in Brooklyn ended just after his relationship did, so now he's here, wearing a silk polo shirt in a room that smells like soup and ointment, wondering how depressing it will be to stay in his dead mother's rented condo for a couple of weeks while he figures out his next move.

His grandma smiles, doesn't reply to the comment about his name. "How's the farm?"

He hasn't been out to it yet and hasn't seen it since he was a kid. It's outside Delmar, in the middle of nowhere. He's not sure how often his mother went there after his grandmother signed the property over to her—Ty and his mom rarely got past small talk the few times a year he remembered to call her back.

"I'm heading there soon," he says, dodging her question. "But I'll pick you up Sunday for the mass, okay? I'll be here at 8:30." He doesn't say "memorial mass."

"That will be lovely, Shep," she says. "I've got the perfect dress. Lavender. With a matching jacket." She pats her permed white hair, faded from its original blonde.

He doesn't say black might be more appropriate. "It'll be fine, Grandma." She looks at him. "I mean it'll look great. You will." He checks his watch.

"Alright," she says. "Well, I'll be ready."

He kisses her cheek and stands to leave, hoping he didn't stay long enough for his clothes to absorb the smell of the place.

§

The next day, he arrives at the farm in his mom's Civic, braced to find a wreck. He's only half right.

The barn is in bad shape, and several smaller outbuildings have collapsed. The yard and pasture are so overgrown that Ty sees six-foot trees among the waist-high grass and brush. The grape field is a tangled mess and the dirt driveway is full of weeds.

Ty steps around pricker plants and something that looks sticky. Tiny green burrs cling to his khakis anyway. When he climbs the stairs to the wide front porch, its floorboards creak but hold. A rusty windchime clanks in the breeze.

The key sticks in the lock and he has to wiggle it before it clicks, then shove his shoulder against the door to get it open. He rubs the sore spot as he pockets the key and walks in, holding his breath.

He exhales.

If not for the dust and cobwebs, he'd believe that someone just ran to the store and would be home to make dinner.

A blue and white afghan lies folded over the back of a beige mohair sofa. A stack of newspapers sits on the coffee table. Dishes are lined up in the drainboard next to the sink. A sign hangs on the kitchen wall, embroidered and framed:

God Bless This Mess.

Ty walks into one of the two bedrooms. A bare mattress takes up space in the middle of the floor and the closet is empty except for a few wire coat hangers. His footsteps leave a trail in the dusty shag carpet.

He tries the bathroom faucet; no water supply. No electricity either. He walks back out to the porch, adding costs in his head. He'll need to hire a service to come mow, mend the pasture fence, fix the caved-in section of barn roof. Clear away the collapsed sheds. Paint. Bring in new gravel for the driveway.

He can use his mom's savings to pay for some of it, and do the easier work himself. If he sells the place for a nice profit, he can get a fresh start in a new city. Chicago, Seattle, or someplace warmer.

He locks the door and whistles as he walks back to the car.

§

For the second time in two weeks, Ty finds himself packing boxes and carrying bags of trash to a dumpster. His mom saved everything—old issues of Reader's Digest, his elementary school art projects, outdated clothing in four sizes. He doesn't see anything worth keeping until he finds the photo album in a box in the hallway closet.

It's full of pictures of the farm, some in color but most in black and white. The album's pages are yellow with age, and spidery handwriting labels each photo in faded brown ink. Ty tells himself he can look through it later, though—

the charity truck will be there at five. He puts the album back in the box and fits the box into the Civic's backseat, next to bags of his own clothing and a few other items he took when his ex kicked him out of their Brooklyn apartment.

By this time the next day, he'll be settled in at the farm.

§

After two days of dusting and vacuuming, playing 90s rock ballads on his phone to break up the solitude of the empty farm, Ty visits his grandmother. He brings the album, figuring it will give them something to talk about—the farm, what it used to look like, how he can restore it or improve it to put it on the market.

When he sets the album on her lap and opens it to the first page, she puts her hand to her mouth and doesn't speak for a whole two minutes. She has to wipe her eyes and clear her throat.

"Oh, would you look at us. Your grandpa and I had the world by the tail." She's staring at the first photo, in black and white, of herself and Ty's grandfather, standing on the porch steps at the farm. In it she looks twenty, the sun shining in her hair, his grandpa a little older, smiling not at the camera but at his wife. The lilac bush next to them is in bloom and chickens peck the dirt nearby.

"I look like him," says Ty, though the longer he studies the picture, the more differences he sees. His grandfather was taller, more broad in the shoulders, hair darker, jaw square. But Ty has the same wide mouth, the same thick eyebrows, the same sharp nose.

His grandmother looks from the picture to Ty and back. "I married the handsomest man in the county. And what a charmer! Those first weeks we were dating. Lord. He made me forget I was Catholic. I knew just what I was doing when I climbed the ladder to that hay loft."

Ty almost says "Gross," but he's looking at the photo too, and realizes he's not seeing his grandparents, but a young couple in love. The way he's looking at her. Of course he invited her to the hay loft. Of course she said yes. Or it could have been the other way around—she invited him.

Ty opens his mouth to ask a question about the farm, but his grandma is staring at the picture, her hand flat on the album page. She seems far away, and a glance at his watch tells him it's getting late. He stands, kisses her head, and walks back to the car.

§

That weekend, the house clean, windows open to the warm July breeze, Ty gives the porch floor a fresh coat of dark green paint. The same lilac bush from the photo is so overgrown now that Ty has to cut it back, using rusty loppers he found in the barn. It still has a few blooms on it, and Ty surprises himself by cutting them free from the shorn branches and putting them in a water glass on the kitchen table. Using the side door, he goes back outside to survey his work. It looks nice, but something is missing. Curb appeal. He remembers a sale on patio furniture at Thurber's, the hardware store where he got the paint.

It takes less than an hour to go back to the store and buy a couple of canvas chairs and a small wooden table, 30% off. On his way to the register he passes a display of windchimes and grabs one shaped like a frog on a lily pad, metal daisies dangling from the bottom. He looks at the tag—not on sale. He buys it anyway, to replace the one that rusted.

§

Back at the house, the porch paint still tacky, he sets up one of the chairs in the shade of the lilac, sits back, and falls asleep. He's not sure how long he's been out when he's awoken by a strange warbling sound, almost like a laugh, but not quite human. He thinks he dreamed it until he catches movement near his feet. It's a chicken.

He stands up, alarmed. He's never been this close to a live one. Then he sees three more—one near the car, one over by the barn, and one leaving footprints like Chinese letters across the fresh paint of the porch floor. They all seem not to notice him.

They must be a neighbor's. There are two other farms along this stretch of road. Ty doesn't know if chickens can be shooed, but he tries. He flaps his arms at the one on the porch, who clucks in fright and runs away, leaving another trail of scratches in the paint. The one next to the car flutters up and perches on the hood. The chicken near the barn runs inside of it through the broken door.

The chicken by his feet doesn't move at all, just turns its head from side to side, looking at him.

"Shit!" he says, to himself and the chickens. He tries again to scare them, to chase them to the road, to chase them back home, but again he fails, and after fifteen minutes, cursing and out of breath, he gives up and goes inside to make dinner. By this time three have escaped into the barn and the other is still on the car. It looks comfortable.

§

Ty spends Sunday breaking apart the three collapsed sheds, hauling the debris in an old wheelbarrow to a cleared patch of dirt, and piling it up to burn. He's seen the chickens, but they remain elusive, clucking and warbling and scattering every time he gets too close to them. He thinks one is still in the barn, but all of them are white so he can't tell them apart.

By early evening, the job is done except for the burning. The pile is too big so Ty has to make a smaller one, starting the fire with old newspaper and feeding pieces from the larger pile onto it. He drags over one of the canvas chairs and sits down, enjoying the crackling noises and the way the fire gets brighter as the sun fades. He's lost in thought when he hears a vehicle pull into the driveway. *Damn*, he thinks. Open burning might not be legal. He should have checked.

A man in his sixties approaches, but he's smiling and wearing a flannel shirt and jeans, not a uniform.

"Saw the fire," he says to Ty. "I'm Brad Evans, your neighbor up the road, at the dairy farm. You must be young Shep. Haven't seen you in decades."

Ty almost corrects him, but it's exhausting to reintroduce himself to all the people who knew him as a child. He gave up at the funeral mass after the tenth woman called him Shep and said she was sorry for his loss and hugged him too hard, all their perfumes mingling on his suit coat so that he'd had to have it dry cleaned. Plus he's not a financial analyst anymore. He's not much of anything these days.

So he says, "Yeah," and shakes Brad's hand, then gestures at the fire. "The smaller sheds all collapsed; figured this would be the cheapest way to get rid of them."

Brad nods. "Nice to see someone cleaning the old place up. Saw your car a few days ago but didn't wanna intrude."

"It's my mother's. Was my mother's. The car," Ty says. "Though I guess it's mine now. The farm too. She passed away recently. My mom."

"Heard about that. I'm real sorry," says Brad, and Ty is relieved that the older man doesn't hug him or even pat him on the back. "So what are you going to do with the place?"

"I'm selling it," Ty says. "I'm not much of a farmer."

One of the chickens wanders out from its hiding place, pecking in the dirt. Another clucks from somewhere in the shadows.

"Then why do you have chickens?" Brad asks, pointing.

"That's not mine," says Ty, holding up his hands like he's been accused of something. "They showed up yesterday and I can't seem to get them to leave."

"Well, not mine," says Brad. "Keep all reds at my farm. Not the McMurrays' either—they're just grapes now, no livestock. But we get a lotta animals dumped out here. Mostly it's cats—got nine in my barn, last count—but not always. Had a goat for ten years that I just found one night in my driveway. Named her Doris Day. She wasn't any trouble."

Ty blinks at Brad for a few seconds, tracing the narrative back to stray chickens. "Well, do you want them?"

"Nope," says Brad. "Can't have the crossbreeding. Just get a sack of chicken feed down at Thurber's tomorrow and throw a few handfuls twice a day. Maybe they'll be good layers. Don't need a rooster—'less you wanna breed them. Gotta check every morning, though, to get the eggs fresh."

Ty is blinking again. "But I don't want them."

Brad laughs and looks at the chicken, who's been joined by another. "Tell them that." He walks back to his truck still laughing.

§

It's early August before Ty gets back to see his grandma. The last weeks have been busy with painting and coordinating repairs. Money is running low. But the barn roof is fixed and new doors have been hung, and Ty even bought a roll of chicken wire and fenced off a section inside for the girls, which is what he's been calling the chickens.

He's learned that if he scatters their food outside in the morning and puts it inside their pen at night, they'll follow it and now they're more or less on a routine. He's gotten twelve eggs and he tells himself they taste better than store bought.

He also tells himself that the eggs are why he's now worried about foxes and counts the girls twice before he locks them in at night, bolting first their pen and then the barn doors.

He's had the white siding pressure washed, and ordered supplies to fix the pasture fence. The grass and brush have been cut and he has a crew coming next week to prune the grapes back, remove dead vines, and repair the posts. It'll ruin most of the grapes growing now, but the field will be ready for next year.

Hopefully that'll attract buyers—growers or people who'll want to lease the fields. He can't afford a load of gravel for the driveway, so that will have to wait, along with other projects—painting the barn, replacing the shutters on the house, and updating the kitchen.

He'll need to sell soon or find another way to make some money.

§

His grandma already has the photo album on her lap when Ty gets to the common room at the nursing home. He stops in the doorway and watches her, noticing the bend of her back and the way her thin hands flutter when she turns a page. She looks somehow smaller every time he visits.

She has the album opened to a page near the middle. He steps around her walker, kisses her hello, and pulls up a chair. Bending his head close, Ty can see that these pictures are from years later than those on the first page—his mother is in them, though she's only a toddler.

One photo shows his grandmother in a lawn chair with his mother on a blanket in the grass nearby, holding a fat, angry-looking cat in her little arms.

"Lynnie was about three here," his grandma says. "She loved every god blessed animal on that farm, even the barn cats. You know, I never wanted to be a mother."

Ty looks up, surprised that she felt this way, or maybe that she's telling him about it. "Oh?" he says, because he can't think of anything else.

"That's why we didn't have more, though your grandpa would have liked to," she says.

She turns the page, and now some of the photos are in color and out of order. There is one of his grandmother blowing out candles on a birthday cake, one of his grandparents at their wedding, and another of his mom at age seven or eight, sitting on the rails of the pasture fence with the flank of a large animal, maybe a horse, just behind her. She's grinning at the camera.

"Not that I didn't love her," his grandma continues. "Of course I did. I just mean you can't always know what will happen. You can't plan for it."

Ty nods, and changes the subject by turning the page. On this one there's a picture of his grandfather, posing in front of the barn and holding up a pine tree as tall as he is. Snow covers the ground.

"Christmas?" Ty asks.

"Mm-hmm. We always went out for our own tree," his grandma says. "That way we could be proud of it."

"Of course," he agrees. The photo is in black and white. "What color was the barn, then?" Now it's barely a color at all—just faded red chips of paint clinging to old boards.

His grandma doesn't pause to think. "Blue," she says. "And I liked it better that way."

"Okay," Ty says. "We can change it. It doesn't have to be red." He looks at his watch and stands to leave, but she grabs his left hand with both of hers.

"You will?" she says, beaming. "I know the color doesn't really matter. It's the same place either way, always will be. I'd love to see it again." She's still holding onto him, but her eyes are back on the photos.

"Sure, Grandma," Ty says, sitting back down. He puts his free hand over both of hers and they sit like that for a minute. "I'll paint it blue and then you can come see it, alright? We can have lunch."

He leaves his grandmother smiling over her pictures and walks back to the parking lot, cursing silently. Why did he promise her that? The only way to have enough money to paint the barn is to cancel the work on the grapes.

§

Less than a week later, Ty gets a call from the nursing home. His grandmother has been getting upset if they try to take her photo album away, at meals and bedtime. Last night she pinched the attendant so hard his skin bruised. The woman on the phone sounds, bizarrely, like she wants an apology from Ty.

"Why are you taking her photo album away?" he asks instead, a surge of anger making his voice louder than he intends. "That's hers."

The woman on the phone pauses, then says, "I see. Well we'll do our best. But perhaps it would help if you came by to talk to her."

"I'll be there first thing in the morning," Ty says, and hangs up without saying goodbye.

He spends a few minutes staring at the pale yellow kitchen wall, realization sinking in. He can't sell the farm and take off for Seattle or LA or anywhere else. He can't leave his grandma. What is she now, eighty? Older? He knows he wasn't a great son. Maybe he can be a better grandson.

That night he takes the last of his belongings out of the trunk of his car and brings them into the house, adding them to the pile in the smaller of the two bedrooms. That sad heap is his whole life—a suitcase bulging with fancy clothes he has no reason to wear, a plastic garbage bag spilling books and old DVDs onto the floor, and the box he took from the closet at his mother's house.

He crouches down to dig through the box now, pulling out his mother's high school diploma, a shabby teddy bear, a bouquet of plastic tulips, and an envelope stuffed with loose photos. He dumps these onto the floor.

It's a jumble of different eras. Wedding photos of his parents and a couple snapshots of his dad, who left before Ty was born. Every school picture of himself, kindergarten through senior year. Candid shots of his mother with friends Ty never met.

And older pictures, too, ones that maybe fell out of his grandmother's album or that never made it in. Some in color, but most, like the others, in black and white.

He picks one up. In it, his grandma looks like a teenager, but maybe she's not that young here. She's sitting on the porch steps at the farm, her mouth open and laughing, her eyes squeezed shut. Ty puts it next to his keys so he can bring it to her tomorrow when he visits.

§

Later, lying in bed, staring at the ceiling, he makes a plan. He'll stop at Thurber's and apply for a part-time job there—he saw a Help Wanted sign the last time he had to buy feed for the girls.

It's just for now, he tells himself, just until his grandma passes away and he can sell the farm. He'll be back to shaking clients' hands in no time.

He practices saying, "Call me Ty, Call me Ty, Call me Ty," into the darkness, and he's almost asleep when he hears a knocking sound.

At first he ignores it, but the knocking becomes louder, more insistent. He gets up and turns on lights, following the sound through the kitchen. It's outside. He flicks the porch light on and sees a fat orange cat. It's slapping at the screen door, bouncing it against the frame. It looks up to meow at Ty.

He groans. Another stray. Well, Brad did warn him. He opens the door to tell the cat to get lost, but it darts between his feet and heads to the living room, where it jumps onto the couch and curls up.

Ty follows it and reaches out to push it onto the floor, hoping to get it back outside, but the cat hisses and swipes at Ty's hand, claws out. Then it closes its eyes. Ty feels dismissed, and goes back to bed. He'll deal with the cat later.

§

When he sees his grandmother the next day, she's hugging her photo album to her chest and scowling. He says hello three times before her eyes focus on him and her shoulders relax.

"They've been taking my things, Shep," she says to him. "They want to take away my pictures."

He tries to soothe her, but he doesn't want to argue. "Maybe they just wanted you to eat, Grandma, or get some sleep. But it's alright. I talked to them and I told them it's yours. Okay? Look, I brought you another picture." He holds the photo he found out to her.

She rests the album on her lap and takes the picture from him, a tremor in her hands. But her voice is strong when she says, "Oh! This is from the day we met. I mean your grandpa and I. I told him not to take my picture, but you did anyway and really I didn't mind."

"You mean Grandpa did."

"That's what I just said! Well, I was out joyriding in my father's Chevy, coasting down back roads like I did whenever he let me borrow the car. And your grandpa had a sign up: Fresh Eggs and Produce. But I didn't stop because of the sign. I stopped because I saw him bent over next to it, pulling tomatoes out of a bushel."

Ty laughs and doesn't check his watch.

"I got out and walked around the car because I wanted him to see me in my new shorts," she says, looking at the photo in her hands. "And I introduced myself and asked him how much for a dozen eggs. Remember what you said?"

"What Grandpa said?"

"Of course Grandpa! He said, 'I'm Shep, and pretty ladies like you pay half price.' Well that worked. We talked for hours and he forgot to give me my eggs but he took my money. I had to come back the next day for them. He did that on purpose."

"I'm sure he did," Ty says, reaching out to give her hand a squeeze. "Listen, the barn is going to be done by the weekend. Why don't I pick you up on Saturday? We can go back to the farm and have lunch."

"That will be wonderful," she says, and when Ty leaves her a few minutes later, she's once again bent over her photo album, smiling.

When he gets home, the cat is still asleep on the couch. Ty shrugs and adds "cat food" to the grocery list on the kitchen counter.

§

The chickens and the mean cat don't seem like such a big deal when Ty is roused at dawn Saturday morning by the sound of braying outside his bedroom window. He stumbles to the porch in his boxer shorts, barefoot and rubbing his eyes, to find a donkey heading toward the barn, which the painters finished the day before. The donkey sees him and brays again.

"This is bullshit," Ty says to the donkey and himself, and goes inside to find Brad's number.

A moment later he's back outside, phone in hand and still not dressed. He calls Brad. "There's a fucking donkey in my yard," he says, almost shouting.

"Shep? That you?" says Brad. He sounds wide awake and cheerful.

"Yes," Ty says. "Sorry. Brad, I woke up to a donkey in my yard. Is it yours? Or maybe the McMurrays'? I can keep the chickens, for now, and I'll feed the damn cat, but this is ridiculous. This is too much."

"Keep your shirt on," Brad says. "If it's got an owner looking, we'll hear about it."

Ty thinks Brad sounds too casual. "What do you mean 'if'? It's a stray donkey."

"Well it could be a Doris Day situation," Brad says. "Though she wasn't any trouble, like I told you."

The donkey takes a few steps closer to Ty and brays in his face, showing Ty all of its teeth. Ty yells and jumps back.

"Sounds hungry," says Brad, still talking like everything's fine. "They like carrots. Got any carrots?"

"No," says Ty. He thinks. "I have a banana."

"That'll do. Have it follow the banana into the pasture and shut the gate."

Ty waits, but Brad doesn't follow that up with anything. "Then what?"

"Well then you'll wanna go down to Thurber's and get it some feed."

Ty ends the call.

§

Within the hour, Ty is on his way to pick up his grandmother. He'll have to make flyers and post the donkey to social media later. It had bitten him in the elbow, then grabbed the banana before walking itself into the pasture.

Ty called it an asshole and cleaned the bite marks with dish soap and warm water. He passed the cat, asleep again on the couch, reluctantly added "donkey food" to the grocery list, and left.

§

His grandma looks good today. Her eyes are bright and she's chatty. She sits in the front seat, commenting on everything she sees out the window—that Thurber's has a bigger sign than it used to, that the sky is bright now but she thinks it will rain later, that there's too much road work going on, that the new sidewalk in front of the library looks nice.

Ty nods along, and when they pull into the driveway at the farm, sending the chickens running toward the porch, she's delighted.

"Shep!" she says. "Everything looks wonderful. I love the barn color. Thank you for fixing it!"

She doesn't seem to notice the other improvements, but then again, she hasn't seen the place in years. Maybe to her, it looks like it always has. And that makes Ty feel good, too. That he put it back to the way it was supposed to be.

"I'm glad you like it," he says. "Grandma, wait just a minute. I'm going to get your walker out of the trunk, okay?" He climbs out and hurries to the back of the car. But when he pulls on the walker, one of its wheels catches in the handles of a canvas grocery bag.

By the time Ty gets it free and shuts the trunk, he looks up to see his grandmother moving toward the donkey, walking unassisted and faster than he thought she could.

"Grandma!" he calls out, dropping the walker in the driveway. "Don't get near it! That thing bites!" He runs to her.

But she's already reaching out to rub the donkey's nose, and it's making an odd nickering sound at her. She whispers and the donkey leans out farther, stretching its neck over the pasture fence and pushing its head into her shoulder. She turns to kiss its nose. Then she looks back, laughing.

"Silly!" she says. "I've told you so many times. Clyde only bites men!" She turns back to the donkey. "Don't you?"

Ty stammers.

"Where are his crackers?" she says. "Do we have any in the pantry?"

Ty nods, confused, but his grandma looks so happy. The donkey does, too.

"Be a dear and get them, will you?"

Ty does, and after the donkey eats three sleeves of Ritz crackers, Ty helps his grandma into the house for sandwiches and iced tea in the kitchen. He makes turkey for himself, and his grandma wants tunafish. He's telling her about how he had to reinforce the chicken wire in the barn when he notices her feeding every other bite of her sandwich to the cat. It's weaving between her feet, purring.

"Grandma, you need to eat your sandwich," he says. "We might not have you back home in time for dinner."

"We're home now! You're being so funny today, Shep," she says. "Plus, tunafish is his favorite."

The cat purrs and his grandma laughs.

Ty lets it go.

§

After cups of decaf coffee on the porch, cat at their feet, Ty drives his grandma back to Twilight Meadow. She sleeps on the way there, and Ty turns off the radio to let her rest. She's so worn out that he has to borrow a wheelchair from the front desk to get her back to her room.

"I'll see you soon, Grandma," he says, pausing in the doorway.

But she's already asleep.

§

The next morning, he gets a phone call from the nursing home director. His grandmother died sometime in the night.

§

By late September, he's learned the register and order forms at Thurber's and been promoted to assistant manager, though that just means he has to do inventory on Thursday nights. He doesn't mind; he still likes working with numbers.

The girls lay more eggs than they used to, and on Saturdays, before poker night at Brad's, he sets up a stand in front of the house: Fresh Eggs and Produce. The "produce" part is a stretch, since all he has to offer now are a few quarts of grapes, salvaged from the wild vines he still can't afford to have trimmed. But people stop to buy them, sometimes.

The cat hasn't gotten any nicer, and no one has claimed the donkey. But every time he gives the cat tunafish and brings crackers out to Clyde, dropping them in a feed tray to avoid the donkey's teeth, he thinks of his grandma and the last time he saw her. How it was a good day.

§

He's sitting in a lawn chair by the driveway on the final Saturday of the month when a muddy pickup pulls over and a woman hops out. Her red hair is tied back in a low bun and she's wearing cutoffs with a gray t-shirt. She smiles at Ty and his mouth goes dry.

"Hi," she says.

"Hi," he says back, too quiet, and stands up. He clears his throat. "Hi," he says again. Her eyes are as green as Clyde's pasture after two days of rain.

"I'm Kelly."

He's still looking at her eyes.

"So…" she says, putting her hands in her back pockets and shrugging her shoulders.

"How much for a dozen eggs?"

And then it clicks.

He remembers his line.

"Oh!" he says. "I'm Shep. And pretty ladies like you pay half price."

PUNCHING IN

Every afternoon Trish checked the clock and willed the hands to move faster. She crossed off the days on a calendar tacked to the cubicle wall by a previous temp worker.

Two weeks at Lakeshore Data Entry felt like a very long time, though her impatience then seems funny to her now. Hilarious.

Because now, days always stop at 4:48 p.m., it's always Friday, and the end of the job—the end of anything—never comes.

§

She thought it was a dream. A nightmare. One of those anxiety episodes: falling through the sky or being pantless in high school or having sex in public. She waited to wake up. But she didn't, so she paid attention, and by the third or fourth day of the same day, Trish understood that she was trapped. Is trapped.

That first Friday, the beginning of the Fridays that never end, she spilled yogurt down her peach-colored blouse during her lunch break. She blotted at it with a wet paper towel, but a whitish smear remained.

The underwire in her cheap bra dug into her rib cage. The G on her keyboard kept sticking and she had to pry it up with the tip of a pencil. By four o'clock she was staring at the water stain above Louis's desk one cubicle over. The yellow-brown blotch was shaped exactly like a spaceship. Is shaped exactly like a spaceship.

The clock ticked past 4:30. Her smile was barely fake when Kenny, the manager, came around. He eyed the yogurt smear on her chest and sucked his mustache, then gave her one of his corny lines: "It's been two weeks already? But we can't let you go that easily!" He chuckled and walked away.

She didn't know he meant it.

She tries to keep track of the days—the repeats, the reruns of this day. But she can't, because every morning, at 9:01 when the day starts over, the Friday on the wall calendar is blank, awaiting the last X. She doesn't know where she goes during the night; the clock reaches 4:48 p.m. but never 4:49; the next tick hits 9:01 a.m., and she's sitting at her desk, and Louis is leaning over the cubicle wall, asking, "So Trisha, do you have any exciting weekend plans?"

And before she can say, "My name is Trish, no A," he cuts her off with, "None for me. Just a little racquetball at the gym," and then Kenny comes by with a stack of papers and thumps it down and says, "Here's our number one employee!" and puts his moustache back in his mouth and walks away.

Over and over.

§

She has willed herself—her hands, her legs, her mouth—to do things differently, thinking if she can, it will break the time loop. But her body isn't hers anymore; she can't seem to control it.

At 9:01 she is always typing, and she always listens politely to Louis, who never says anything new and neither does Kenny, and her head nods and her lips smile and her words stay trapped, and the G key sticks and sticks and sticks.

She has typed in this particular stack of forms so many times that she does it now without looking at the papers or the screen: 265749 CTSCN APPR

Belinda F. Renald, enter. 784790 AMPLG APPR Simon P. Shultz, enter. She stares around her dull prison.

The walls are an anonymous greige, the color of a smudge. The carpet used to be blue, and curls up in the far corner. A dusty fake plant sits next to the copy machine, which doesn't work.

Three other people sit in three other cubicles, but Trish never bothered to ask their names and now she can't.

§

She has wondered if she is dead. If this is a residual haunting. She watched a documentary about it once. The ghosts are just old records that play and play. Echoes, nothing more. But she has a papercut on her right pinky and it stings when she hits "Shift" and "Enter." Could a ghost feel that? Or the poking underwire? She thinks probably not.

§

On day 467 or day 46,007, a breakthrough.

Louis leans over the cubicle wall. He says, "So Trisha, do you have any exciting weekend plans?" And though her mouth cannot form the words to correct him, it opens, and her throat loosens enough to make a noise.

A strangled, ugly noise, but they both hear it. She stares at Louis and he stares back. Then he smooths his combover and sits down, not mentioning racquetball at all.

She wonders, now—throat aching from its effort, chest rising with unspent sound—what else she can change.

§

Days later—or is it only one day?—Louis leans over. He says, "So Trisha, do you have any exciting weekend plans?"

And before he gets to "None," she does it—in a voice rusty as old pipes, she grinds out, "My name is Trish." The effort costs her; pain flares in her throat. She's happy to pay and finishes her thought: "No A."

She feels a trickle of wetness on her lower lip, tastes salt and iron. Blood.

Louis looks like he's going to vomit and sits down.

When Kenny comes around in the afternoon, when he says, like always, that he won't let her go, she is ready, fists clenched beneath her desk. She knows this will hurt. She locks her eyes onto his, takes a deep breath, and screams.

Before this moment, the scream only lived in her head. But this time, she is sure, it is out loud. It spews 468 or 46,008 days of held-back rage. Maybe more. Maybe decades. A lifetime. Generations.

It startles Louis, who falls out of his chair. The heads of the other workers swivel in her direction. A bubble of bloody saliva forms on her lips and pops, spattering her blouse, her keyboard, with pink flecks.

Then she smiles, this time showing Kenny all her teeth.

He walks away, hurrying, almost jogging. He's not laughing now and his moustache goes un-sucked.

§

It's 4:46. The second hand is doing its slow spin. The office is quiet, just fingers tapping keyboards and the low hum of the ancient heating system. Trish watches the clock.

This could be it.

POOR BILLY

When Drew's dad, tired and cranky then like he was every night since being promoted to manager at Dollar Central, yelled at his son to clean up his toys and then mumbled about someone called Poor Billy—*he'll take your stuff/he'll appreciate it/think your life is so hard/you ungrateful little bastard*—Drew tried to ignore him.

Drew was twelve. Old enough to know that ignoring his dad was a bad idea. Old enough to do it anyway.

He tried to slip past his father and into his bedroom, the one he shared with his little brother, Pete. But his dad grabbed him by the shoulder and added pressure until it hurt. Drew tried to twist away but couldn't.

When his mom rushed in from the kitchen and told them to knock it off, Drew ran to his room, slammed the door, and covered his ears. It muffled his parents' yelling and the crash that followed—probably his mom throwing her drink again.

Pete bawled from his spot on the floor, where he'd been stacking blocks. Drew pressed his hands harder against the sides of his head and waited.

When things got quiet, he uncovered his ears.

That's when his dad pushed the bedroom door open and stood with his arms stretched across the frame. "You still haven't picked up your toys like I asked you to," he said. His voice was angry but quiet, and it scared Drew, who didn't move or answer.

His dad took that as a challenge. "Fine," he said, and looked around the room, at the ceiling, into the corners. "Poor Billy!" he called. "Help yourself! Drew doesn't want his toys."

Then he walked down the hall, laughing the way he did when things weren't really funny.

§

Drew stayed in his room all evening, pretending to be asleep when his mom staggered in to put Pete to bed. When Drew woke up the next day, he found Pete watching Saturday morning cartoons, his mom in the kitchen swallowing aspirin, and his father gone.

Drew sighed with relief, then noticed his toys—the action figures and comic books his dad had yelled about—were gone too.

When his father got home late in the afternoon, Drew watched him remove his tie and nametag, then hang his button-up shirt in the closet. His dad was pulling at his shoelaces by the time Drew worked up the courage to say he couldn't find his things; that he was sorry he didn't pick them up the night before, but could he have them back? His dad looked confused before his face settled into its usual irritated expression.

"You're kidding me, right?" he asked Drew. "You lost them? Really? Just like your retainer last year? And the jacket we bought you for Christmas?" He sighed and rubbed his forehead. "First you throw your stuff around the apartment, and now you're saying it's gone? Lost? Goddammit, Drew!"

"No!" Drew said, but worry made his voice high pitched—even to himself, it sounded like he was lying. "No," he said again. "They were here but now they aren't. It's *not* like my retainer. I swear! I thought you—"

"You thought I'd what? Help you find the stuff you lost? The stuff *I* bought? Or did you think I'd replace it? Buy it all brand new? You know, I keep telling your mother. This promotion doesn't mean we can piss away money. You have to take *care* of your things. You have to *learn*." Still wearing his work khakis, he pushed past Drew and went into the living room. A moment later Drew heard the T.V. click on.

He knew it. His dad was *teaching him a lesson*. His dad loved to teach lessons. He loved to say *that'll teach you* and *now you know* and *bet you won't do that again*.

Drew went to the kitchen and found his mom. It was early enough that she'd only had a few drinks. But when he told her what happened, what his dad had done, she just shook her head. "Drew," she said. "Come on. Your dad wouldn't do that."

"He would," said Drew. "He did!"

"Stop it," she said, and set her empty wine glass on the counter. "And if this is about your dad, why are you coming to me? I know he likes to play the martyr but he's not the only one who's stressed out."

She turned away from him and refilled her glass. When she didn't say anything else, Drew stomped to his room. He sat on his bed, fought tears, and lost.

He buried his face in his pillow. Everything felt so unfair—his dad's attitude, his mom's cluelessness, even Pete's constant fussing. It was all so wrong and broken and sad, but no one was doing anything about it. Including him.

Because Drew couldn't make his dad's job easier. He couldn't stop his mom's drinking or his parents' fighting. He couldn't really keep his little brother from crying, except for when Drew played blocks or cars with him, which he secretly liked to do—when Pete was happy, he was pretty fun to be around. Still, Pete cried a *lot*.

But there was something Drew could do, he realized. He could catch his dad—prove it was him taking Drew's toys to teach some dumb lesson Drew didn't need to learn in the first place.

Go to his mom and tell her everything, make her see, make her pay attention to him for once.

He just needed a plan.

§

By late Sunday night, he was ready.

While his dad sat on the couch watching a baseball game, Drew gathered a set of plastic blocks and snuck into the living room, placing them one by one on the worn runner that led to the kitchen. His dad would see them the next time he got up for a drink or snack.

Drew hoped he'd step on one barefoot. It would serve him right.

After waiting a few minutes to make sure his dad didn't notice him, Drew tiptoed back to his room, where Pete was already asleep. Drew's plan was to leave the door open a crack and sit up in the dark with a flashlight. He'd watch his dad steal his stuff, then flick on the flashlight, yell "Gotcha!," and holler for his mom.

But it's hard to wait in the dark, and before long Drew's eyes closed and his head fell back against his bed. He woke up in the morning chilly and sore, sprawled on the thin carpeting of his bedroom.

Crap, he thought.

He got up, rubbed his eyes, and hurried to the living room to check on his blocks. They were gone.

His mom sat at the kitchen table, leaning over a cup of coffee. "Is Dad at work already?" he asked her.

"Yep," she said, not looking up. "One of his employees called in sick. He had to open the store."

Drew sighed and headed toward the bathroom to get ready for school. He was going to have to try harder.

§

The idea came to Drew that afternoon, when he got home and saw Pete playing with his farm toy. It was shaped like a barn and had different buttons that made animal sounds when Pete pressed them. Drew needed something like that—something that made noise.

He had just the thing. That night, he would leave out the motion-activated robot his aunt had sent him for his last birthday. It walked and talked and had a light-up circuit board on its chest. He'd just have to put fresh batteries in it, and remember to turn it on. That way, if he did fall asleep, the noise would wake him up as soon as his dad reached down to grab it.

§

It almost worked. He heard the robot say, "What is my next task?" in its computer voice, but it took a second for Drew to wake up all the way and when he tried to turn on his flashlight, the beam was weak and died a second later, just as Drew swept it out into the hallway. He caught movement there, but by the time he flicked on the overhead light, the hall was empty.

Drew put his ear against his parents' closed bedroom door and listened. He heard his father's snore. Back in his own room, Pete lay quietly, too, clutching his favorite stuffed pig. The whole apartment, maybe the whole building, was asleep.

Maybe he'd dreamed it, Drew thought. He gave in to his sleepiness and got into bed.

§

On the third night, Drew saw him.

Drew had spent the afternoon planning, trying to correct his mistakes from the previous two nights. He put new batteries in his flashlight, and instead of leaving a toy in the hallway, he left it right in his bedroom doorway, with the door wide open.

This time he chose his old Hungry Hungry Hippos game, because of how loudly the marbles in it rattled around. Before bed, he raided his mom's stash of chocolate caramels and ate most of them.

He felt wired. Wide awake.

So when he heard the marbles in his game roll and clank like someone grabbed the box, he flicked on his flashlight immediately. And screamed.

It wasn't his dad, or his mom.

It was a little boy. But he looked wrong—all crooked lines and blurred edges. Like someone had done a bad job coloring in a picture. His eyes were black holes in deep sockets, and a bashed-in cheekbone made the yellowish skin of his face sag on one side.

Drew closed his eyes and kept screaming. A moment later his bedroom light flashed on and his dad was at his side. When Drew looked again, the boy was gone but so was the hippo game.

His mom shuffled in next and picked up Pete, who was already awake and crying.

"Dad!" Drew said. "You were right!"

"Right?" his dad said. He was half asleep, rubbing his face. "What's going on? Right about what?"

"Poor Billy!" Drew said. "He's real. He was here!"

His mom bounced Pete a few times and put him back down. He was still sniveling. "Who swhere?" she said, slurring the words together.

"Poor Billy!" said Drew.

Drew's mom looked at her husband. "Whasse talking about?" she asked.

"Nothing," said his dad. He looked at his wife. "Nothing. Go back to bed."

"But whass—"

"Nothing! Go to bed!"

She left but Pete started up again.

"Oh for Christ's sake," said his dad. He picked up Pete. "Okay. Now what's going on? Tell me."

"I'm sorry, Dad," Drew said, talking fast. "Before—I thought you were lying. I thought you were taking my stuff. That you made up Poor Billy. I thought I could catch you and tell Mom and make her listen for once."

His dad continued to look at him.

"But it wasn't you. It was him. It was *him*."

His dad sat down on the bed, moving Pete to his knee. He ran his free hand through his graying hair and sighed.

"Look, Drew," he started. "I shouldn't have mentioned that old story. It's just something—"

"It's not a story!" said Drew.

"Quiet!" said his dad. Pete was nodding off again. "It *is* a story." He stood to put Pete in his toddler bed and made sure the safety rail was locked in place. "My dad—Grandpa Bob—used to threaten me with it—that I'd better pick up my toys or he'd offer them to Poor Billy. Grandpa said Poor Billy didn't have any toys of his own, that he'd take ungrateful kids' playthings if parents called him. It worked on me. Scared me shitless. But I was younger than you. I guess I thought with you being older—but I was pissed off and I shouldn't have—"

"No, Dad," Drew argued. "I *saw* him."

"You had a nightmare," his dad said. He moved to the doorway. "Now, we all need some sleep. You've got school in the morning and I have a long day of inventory ahead of me. Let's get back to bed."

Before Drew could answer, his dad shut off the light and was gone.

§

Drew couldn't fall asleep. He kept picturing the boy he caught in the beam of his flashlight. How he looked back at Drew even though he didn't seem to have eyes.

Drew shivered, listening hard for any odd sounds. He kept his head turned toward the dark doorway.

After what felt like hours, he drifted off.

§

Drew woke up groggy the next morning. Even with his bedroom window cracked open and a breeze coming through, the air felt thick and wet, and his sheets were damp with sweat. He looked at his alarm clock. He was supposed to be at school in an hour.

But he wasn't going to school that day. He was going to the library.

If he couldn't count on his parents—not to believe him, not even to listen—then he would just have to take care of things himself.

And that meant getting rid of Poor Billy.

§

He only had to search Google hits for about ten minutes before he found it: "How to Banish an Unwanted Entity" from a site called simplespells.com. The directions didn't seem hard.

To banish a spirit, you must first call it to you. Light five green candles. Next, take five petals from a red rose and burn them, one per candle. After that, prick your thumb and let the blood drip onto each candle without dousing the flames, and chant the following words:

*"Gods of this world and the next,
with your sight may I be blessed
to see the hidden wraith who roams
throughout these rooms that are my home.
Grant me strength to call then banish
the lost who linger, trouble must vanish."*

Finally, kill the flames with the juice of a lemon. Your house will be cleansed.

Drew paid a quarter to print the spell and directions. After leaving the library, he stopped at a corner deli to grab a ham sandwich. He took it to a nearby park and found a spot on a bench, next to an old man feeding pigeons.

Drew chewed and watched the birds peck at the ground. He went over supplies he needed in his head: candles, rose petals, lemon. Candles, rose petals, lemon. Then he looked up, and grinned.

A yellow rose bush, in full bloom, grew on a low fence near the park's bathrooms and water fountain. Drew took it as a sign that things would work out, that luck was on his side.

He stuffed the rest of his sandwich in his mouth and tried to walk casually to the water fountain. He slurped water for a few seconds, then wiped his mouth and turned toward the roses. A small sign near the ground read "Do not pick flowers."

But Drew had to have those petals.

He crouched down, pretending to tie his shoe, and looked around to make sure no one was watching. Then he broke off a bloom low on the plant and stuffed it in his coat pocket, wincing at a sharp pain in his finger.

He held it up and saw a drop of blood ooze to the surface. Of course; the rose had thorns. Drew smiled, thinking of the spell: *prick your thumb and let the blood drip onto each candle.* The thorns would save him from having to find a needle or a knife.

He wasted another hour walking around the city, and when he thought it was late enough to go home and tell his mother he had a half day, he headed back to the apartment. He found everything quiet when he crept in; his mom and Pete were both asleep in her bed, and his dad was still at work.

He walked quietly into the kitchen and searched the junk drawer, finding what he knew would be there—five half-burnt green-and-white striped birthday candles, plus a book of matches. Next he went to the fridge. No lemons. But the cupboard held powdered lemonade mix, and Drew thought that would work.

He mixed up a glass, careful not to clink the spoon when he stirred. Then he stashed everything under his bed. All he had to do now was wait for a chance to put the spell to use.

And clean up his toys.

Drew didn't want to chance Poor Billy showing up before things were ready. He stacked his comic books on his nightstand, shoved his action figures into the closet, and filled his backpack with drawing supplies.

He didn't have too many board games, and he found room for them under his bed.

Then he looked at Pete's side of the room. Stuffed animals and toddler toys littered the carpet around Pete's bed. His little brother was a pain, but Drew loved him. If the spell didn't work, he didn't want Poor Billy coming after Pete's things.

So Drew put Pete's books back on his bookshelf, tossed his toys in a laundry basket, and threw his stuffed animals onto his bed.

Satisfied, Drew went into the living room to watch T.V.

§

Drew's break came two days later. In that time, there'd been no sign of Poor Billy. No noises at night, no toys gone missing. His parents told him they were going to the Davises' apartment across the hall for drinks after they put Pete to bed. They'd take the baby monitor with them.

"We're close by if you need anything," his dad said. "Come get us or just holler over the baby monitor. I'll lock the door behind me, but remember, don't open it for any strangers."

"I know, I know," Drew told them. They went to the Davises' at least once a month and told him the same thing every time.

As soon as they were out the door Drew moved the baby monitor to the kitchen table so his parents wouldn't hear anything. He raced to his bedroom and pulled out his supplies. The rose had wilted and some of the lemonade had evaporated, but Drew didn't think that would matter.

He realized he needed to stick the candles in something, though, so he ran to the kitchen and took a cup of cherry gelatin from the fridge.

Back in his room, he made sure Pete was still asleep. Then he peeled the foil top off the gelatin and stuck the candles in it. He lit them with a match, then unplugged Pete's nightlight.

Next, he held the wilted rose petals over the flames, using two pencils like chopsticks so he didn't burn himself. After that came the hard part.

He took a deep breath and clenched the rose stem in his left hand, leaving four different punctures in his fingers. It hurt. He squeezed his thumb first, forcing out tiny drops of blood and dripping them onto the flames. When that wouldn't bleed anymore he squeezed the small wounds in his pointer finger. The candles sputtered but didn't go out.

Drew unfolded the paper the spell was printed on, and read the words in his most serious voice. But as soon as he got to "vanish," his bedroom light clicked on. His dad stood in the doorway, baby monitor in one hand and keys in the other. Drew had been so focused that he hadn't heard the front door open.

"Drew! What do you think you're doing?!" his dad said.

Drew opened his mouth to explain, but his dad crossed the room in two strides, tossed his keys on Drew's bed, picked up the cup of gelatin and blew out the candles.

"You know you're not allowed to play with matches!" he said. "And Jesus Christ, right next to your brother? You could burn down the whole goddamn building with all of us in it!"

His shouting woke up Pete, who wailed.

Drew considered telling his dad the truth. About the spell, and what he was trying to do. To keep them all safe. But one more look at his dad's face told him there was no use.

"I wanted to try a science experiment," Drew said, thinking fast. "I'm sorry."

His dad had set the monitor and gelatin cup on Drew's nightstand and picked up Pete to shush him.

"No fire, period," said his dad, glaring at him. "Never. Under any circumstance. And you *know* that. You're grounded for a month."

"Fine," said Drew. He felt miserable. Tears welled and then fell. Not only was he grounded, but his dad ruined the ceremony. How was Drew going to get the supplies to try it again? His dad would hide every match and candle in the house.

"Unbelievable," his dad continued, talking more to himself now. Pete was settling down. "I come back to grab your mother's wine and I find this? I work a sixty-hour week and I get *this* bullshit on my day off?"

He looked at Drew again, waiting for a response. Drew had nothing to say.

"I'm going back to the Davises'," his dad said. He picked up the book of matches and put it in his pocket. "This time, keep the baby monitor ON. I'll be listening."

Drew nodded.

His dad gave him one last angry look, then flipped off the bedroom light and stormed into the kitchen. A moment later Drew heard his dad's footsteps in the hallway, then the front door slam.

§

Left in the darkness, Drew took a few deep breaths, trying to think of what to do next. Nothing came to him. He walked toward his bed and felt around for his lamp, flicking it on.

He wasn't alone.

Poor Billy stood just inside the doorway, his mouth twisted in a lopsided smile. "Hello," he said.

His voice sounded far away, like a fading echo, and the broken half of his face didn't move.

Drew was too scared to scream. He barely felt the warm spread of urine soaking through his pants.

Poor Billy spoke again. "Thanks for inviting me."

Drew stared, noticing what he hadn't before—purple bruises around Poor Billy's neck, a missing patch of hair near his left ear. Ruined hands. Torn pajamas and naked, dirty feet.

"Poor Billy?" Drew said. His voice was a weak thread.

Poor Billy nodded. The motion seemed fast and slow at the same time.

Drew glanced at his sleeping brother and forced his body to move, to get between Pete and the horrible thing in the doorway.

Then he swallowed, trying to find his courage. His voice was a little stronger when he said, "I called you here to banish you. But my dad messed it up."

"Banish?" said Poor Billy. "But I like it here. So many things to play with."

Drew balled his shaking hands into fists. "But they're mine," he said.

"Not after I take them," said Poor Billy. His head turned, both fast and slow, toward Pete.

"It must be fun to have a brother to play with," he said.

"I've always had to play alone." Then he was behind Drew, standing too close to Pete, leaning over him.

Drew whirled around. He hadn't seen Poor Billy move.

"A brother would be better than a toy," Poor Billy continued. He reached for Pete.

Pricks of ice ran up Drew's neck. "No," he whispered. Fresh tears filled his eyes.

"We could play games."

"No."

"Hide and Seek."

"No!"

"Yes." Poor Billy wrapped filthy, broken fingers around Pete's arm.

"Stop!" Drew said. Panic clutched his stomach and his limbs felt like water. "Not Pete!"

His little brother woke up then, screeching like an alarm.

Drew remembered the baby monitor. "Dad! Mom! Help!" he shouted.

Poor Billy pulled the screaming toddler close and picked him up. Drew tried to grab his brother's waist but Poor Billy was quicker, moving away.

Pete reached back for Drew. Shrieking, terrified.

Their parents' voices cut through the noise, calling Drew's name, then Pete's, pounding on the front door.

Drew checked his bed.

His dad had forgotten his keys.

Poor Billy turned, looking back at Drew with those empty sockets. "We need to be going," he said. "Thank you." He flickered, winking in and out like a failing light bulb.

Pete flickered too.

"Help!" screamed Drew, sobbing. Flushes of nausea rolled through his body. The spell. This was all his fault.

"Drew!" his dad yelled. "Pete! Boys!" It sounded like he was kicking the door, trying to break it down.

He wouldn't get there in time.

Pete's face had gone purple. His legs kicked at Poor Billy.

"Wait!" Drew said.

Poor Billy stopped, became more solid. Pete did too.

Drew took a deep breath. "What about me?"

"You?"

Drew looked at his brother. Pete was so small. He looked back at Poor Billy. "I could play with you."

Poor Billy seemed to think about it.

"We can play games," said Drew. "Please!"

"Whatever I want?"

"Anything!"

Poor Billy smiled and dropped Pete on the floor. Pete rolled onto his stomach, gulping for air, pulling himself toward Drew.

"Drew! Pete!" More pounding. More voices.

Poor Billy held out his hand, snapped pinky dangling.

Drew hesitated.

"You or him," said Poor Billy.

"Boys!" Sirens.

"Decide," said Poor Billy.

Pete clutched Drew's ankle, pudgy fingers digging in. Drew looked down, then closed his eyes.

"Drew!"

No time.

"Drew!"

He loved his brother.

"*Drew!*"

He shook Pete off, opened his eyes, and took Poor Billy's hand.

REST FOR THE WICKED

You rent the two-room cottage up by Schroon Lake because it's been a hard year and you just need a little quiet. A little break. You can't sleep in the city and out here maybe you can turn off all the voices.

That first night you're high on all the clean air and you doze off, a half-smile on your face, when something outside breaks the silence. A cat, out for hunting or loving.

It hisses and it yowls and it screams.

Now you're up, restless, and your cruel memory replays that morning in fourth grade when you stole Melissa Ferra's lunch and ate it in the bathroom and blamed that dirty, poor kid named Adam and he got in trouble because there was never a moment he didn't look hungry.

You reclaim a few hours of fitful sleep before dawn pokes you awake again.

§

The next night, belly full of baked beans and barbequed chicken, you doze off, happy you took that three-mile hike and enjoyed the scenery and tired yourself out so now you can sleep.

But a second cat seems to have joined the first, out for fighting or loving or both.

They hiss and they yowl and they scream.

Now you're up, restless, and your cruel memory replays that afternoon in college when you stole the biology test answers from Professor Crenshaw's unlocked office and when he found them missing you told him it was Rita Stonefoot, because she was smart and competent and wouldn't go out with you. Crenshaw believed you and Rita had to retake the test, crying the whole time.

You reclaim a couple hours of fitful sleep before dawn pokes you awake again.

§

The third night, head and lungs clear from a day spent fishing on the river but catching nothing, you doze off, reasoning that you don't like fish that much anyway and the hotdogs you roasted were good if a little burnt. It's the activity that counts, the experience.

But a third cat seems to have joined the others, out for feasting or brawling or loving or more.

They hiss and they yowl and they scream.

Now you're up, restless, and your cruel memory replays that evening in your late twenties at the firm's holiday party at a rented house in the Hamptons when after too many martinis you found yourself alone in an upstairs study with Maude from payroll, drunk herself and just too delicious in that pencil skirt and she did say no but you were sure she'd change her mind, and after a few minutes it didn't matter anyway. You finished on her stomach and threw down cab fare and left her alone to clean herself up.

You reclaim an hour of fitful sleep before dawn pokes you awake again.

§

The fourth night, senses muffled by Canadian whiskey, sunburned skin pulsing from a day spent sitting by the water's edge shirtless, you doze off, thinking of how you only have a few more days in this sylvan paradise before you need to head back to the city and to rush hour and to bodies clogging the dirty sidewalks.

But more cats have joined the others; you count six or seven different cries now, out for God knows what, so many that you get up to peer through the open window's screen and see their slinking bodies dark in the dim moonlight and then they're facing the cottage. They line up to look back at you. A tremor shakes your hand as you draw the curtain but it's too hot to shut the window and you lie in bed sweating and twisting and sweating.

The cats hiss and they yowl and they scream.

Now you're up, restless, and your cruel memory replays that dark night ten years ago when you were heading back from the meeting in Hoboken where you lost the Myers account and a Toyota full of whooping teenagers passed you too close and almost dinged your Jag and of course you answered the challenge, speeding up and cutting them off around that dogleg bend. You saw the truck sail off the edge of the embankment and the flames were clear in your rearview mirror but that's what they got, you told yourself, for reckless driving.

You don't sleep at all and then dawn taunts you, ears ringing, eyes stinging, heartburn lighting up your chest.

§

The fifth night, lying on your back and staring at nothing, your sober guts churning, your tired mind clumsy and dull, you try to doze off but not even fitful sleep will come.

There's a scratching at the window, and at first you think you imagine it, or that perhaps it is a dream, that maybe sleep showed mercy after all, but then the scratching is followed by a tearing and you know this isn't one of your nightmares.

The cats are inside.

And they hiss and they yowl and they scream and they bite and they claw and they flay and they punish and they do not stop until they, and you, are finished.

DAMP IN THE WALLS

Jen had wanted this house with a desperation that squeezed the breath from her chest. Kevin had scoffed at first—for that price, it must be a dump, he'd said. He'd called it a shit-hole. He'd said they would be better off biding their time, renting for another year, saving their money. Then they could see what was what.

But Jen had persisted. She'd done the math. A year's rent would cost them over fourteen grand. If they could pull together five grand, right now, they could get a bank loan for the rest, even with an as-is property, maybe with their parents' help, and loan payments would be $550 a month, give or take.

Kevin was a roofer—surely that meant he could fix other things? Wasn't it all just hammers and nails and paint?

No, he had told her. It was wiring and plumbing and if the foundation was bad, they may as well knock the goddamned thing down, and what the hell did she mean? Just hammers and nails?

Did she only see him as some dumb fuck, banging away eight hours a day at plywood and shingles? And what made her so high and mighty? Was being a cashier at Target really so fucking royal? So fucking fancy?

And the dishes had crashed and a chair had been kicked over and her jaw had been bruised, and so many tears and apologies later he'd said yes, yes they could buy the craftsman at the end of Hayebrook Road next to the winding creek and fix it up and start over and paint every room in her favorite colors and Jen could buy brand-new appliances and he was just sorry sorry so fucking sorry.

She'd held his head to her chest and hushed his crying and the words "start over start over start over" had played through her mind like a frantic lullaby.

§

Only a month later and here they were, the shabby furniture that had filled their apartment bunched on the sagging porch. Jen thought it looked like someone was being evicted, not moving in. But they'd only had Kevin's pickup, and when the rain had come, they'd rushed to unload everything and get it under cover.

Standing in the yard, Jen shivered in her t-shirt but didn't complain—she told herself this was a happy day. She made Kevin pose for a picture by the "Sold" sign near the road, even getting him to smile.

She knew it was fake, but kissed him anyway, buoyed by thoughts of planting tomatoes between the house and the narrow creek that curled around it, blue hydrangeas to flank the steps, tulips by the mailbox. Of painting the kitchen a bright apple green. Of all the extra space—three bedrooms! She could turn one into a library.

"And you could use the third bedroom for an office, for when you start your own roofing company," Jen thought out loud at Kevin, knowing the subject always cheered him.

Since they'd met five years ago, he'd talked about how one day, he was going to tell his boss to shove it and go off on his own, take the customers and a few other employees with him and have so many jobs they couldn't keep up with the bidding.

Jen always smiled, always told him he could do it, that it was going to be great.

"That's right!" he said, warming to the topic like usual. "And you can keep the books for us." He slapped her ass and laughed. They both turned back toward the house.

Jen looked at him, searching his face for the shadows she often saw there. As he gazed at their new home, rainwater beading on his forehead, blackening his already dark hair, running down his cheeks, there were none. She took a deep breath and let it out. Then she looped her arm through his and they climbed the front steps.

"Got the keys?" he asked her.

She pulled them out of her jeans pocket and reached for the brass door handle, ready to stick the heaviest key into the lock. But the door creaked open at the touch of her hand, revealing the entryway and carved wooden staircase. She looked back at Kevin, worry cutting a line across her forehead.

He smiled. "It's no big deal, babe," he said. "The realtor probably forgot to lock it last time she was here."

And then her worries were forgotten, because Kevin swept her off her feet and carried her through the door, crossing the warped floorboards of the foyer and the empty living room and turning the corner into the dim kitchen where he set her on the counter and pulled off her wet clothes with hands Jen had almost forgotten could be that gentle.

By the time the rain stopped they were lying naked on the dusty linoleum, Jen's head on Kevin's chest, Kevin blowing lazy smoke rings into the air above her.

"I love you," she said, and his arm tightened around her back.

§

Kevin worked days, plus overtime when he could get it. Jen worked the closing shift three days a week and doubles on Sundays. Saturdays, the two tackled projects together, sometimes asking Kevin's friends for help.

But Jen spent weekday mornings and afternoons alone in the rambling house, cleaning and prepping and painting what she could. At first, it was fun.

Two weeks in, wearing a paint-flecked tank top and a red bandana to tie back her curly blonde hair, she peeled wallpaper in the living room with a steel putty knife.

The wallpaper felt damp to the touch and came off in easy strips, like sunburned skin that was halfway healed. She had set up her old boombox next to the only wall outlet, a *Best of Madonna* CD playing on repeat.

It was satisfying, seeing the wall's stained surface steadily freed from the tacky rose-and-violet print.

But as the curling pieces piled at her feet, Jen noticed a smell—faint at first, growing stronger. Mildew. It caught in her nose and stuck.

She assumed it was the old wallpaper itself, but two hours in, with the longest wall bare, she bagged up the peelings and took them out to the trash can and came back in and the smell slapped at her like a strong current.

She gagged and backed into the foyer to prop open the front door. The place just needed some air. The living room window didn't open; that was the problem. It was mid-September.

Jen pulled on a faded sweatshirt of Kevin's and welcomed the cool breeze that swept in through the entryway. It eased the smell but didn't chase it away completely.

In the kitchen, most of the old flooring and half of the cabinets had been torn out, but the sink still worked. Jen filled a bucket with hot water and added bleach, found a sponge in a pile of cleaning supplies, and attacked the living room wall.

The antiseptic smell was an improvement, and, switching the Madonna CD for a 90s radio station, she got to work on the other wallpapered section. Thankfully, two of the walls had only been painted.

But the mildew smell crept back, washing into Jen's nose and then her throat. This second wall showed more water stains than the first, swirling and blooming across the plaster, like a tie-dyed mural in only yellows and browns. Jen breathed through her mouth, once again bagged up and got rid of the wallpaper strips, and fetched a fresh bucket of bleach water.

At 12:30, she realized she'd missed lunch and had to hurry to get to work by two. But she was proud of her progress; both long walls in the living room were stripped and scrubbed, the floor had been swept, and after a few cracks were patched, she could start priming.

With paint colors they chose and their own prints and photos on the walls, she told herself, the place would feel more like home.

When she got back that night at 10:30, Kevin told her the living room stunk so bad he had to eat his Chinese takeout on the porch. She told him about the walls, and he promised to pick up a bucket of sealant the next day.

"These old houses," he said. "You have to expect problems. Especially when there's been water damage."

§

By early October, Jen missed her period. Kevin usually pulled out, but if it felt too good, he said, he couldn't make it. Before November, a doctor confirmed she was pregnant. A week later, a judge pronounced Jen and Kevin married at the courthouse, their parents looking on.

No child of his would be a bastard, Kevin promised, and Jen felt a spreading warmth whenever she said the words "my husband" or "our family." Plus, she was thirty-one. Kevin was thirty-six. Wasn't it time?

Naturally, they'd use the bedroom that would have been a library for the baby's room. "My stuff is already in the other one," Kevin reasoned, "and we'll need that space for when we start the family business. After all, that's how I'm going to provide for us."

Jen loved that he wanted to take care of them. That he would teach their child a trade. That they were all in this together. She didn't care about having a library anymore; her books could just as easily take up space in the living room or their bedroom or the attic crawlspace.

§

Jen kept the windows open despite the frost on the lawn. She had to get the baby's room finished so they could bring in the crib and the dresser and some throw rugs, but the walls wouldn't dry.

She'd painted them three days before, choosing a delphinium blue that Kevin had called "dangerously close to purple." But he'd been good to her lately, hurrying to finish the kitchen to make things easier on her.

Jen brushed her fingertips along the wall by the closet door—she knew it was the first one she did. Still, she pulled her hand back to see blue smudges, fresh and wet as paint in a can.

"Shit," she whispered. Kevin wanted to put the flatpack furniture together that night, after he got home. Well, she reasoned, they would just have to keep it away from the walls for now. They could move it later.

§

Mid-January, just after three a.m. Jen woke to the sounds of rushing water, of sloshing, of gurgling somewhere downstairs.

"Fuck!" she said. "Kevin!" and shook him awake. "I knew we should have replaced the pipes!"

Kevin sat up next to her, rubbing his face. She heard his wedding ring rasp against the stubble on his chin. "What?" he asked.

"What's wrong? What pipes?"

"Downstairs! Can't you hear that? It has to be the basement. Shit shit shit." She flung off the covers and sat up, reaching for her robe on a nearby chair. They couldn't afford to fix broken pipes. They couldn't afford to replace them. They had hoped the pipes would hold until they got their tax return in the spring.

"No, I'll go," he said. "Stay here."

A moment later he was pounding down the wide wooden staircase, then, fainter, Jen heard him open the basement door off the kitchen and descend lower. She pushed a pillow behind her back and hugged her growing belly, wondering how the hell they were going to deal with a flooded basement.

They'd had to spring for additional insurance, being next to the creek. But would it cover broken pipes? Or would that be the regular policy? What if the claim got denied? She tried to remember what was being stored down there.

Leftover floor tiles from the kitchen. Paint cans. A couple of window unit air conditioners. Would they be ruined? Kevin had put the washer and dryer up on pallets. Were they high enough?

She tried not to cry.

A few minutes later, walking slower, Kevin returned, not saying anything until he was back in bed next to her.

"Well?" she said. "How bad is it?"

"Go to sleep, Jen," he said. "There's nothing wrong with the basement. Come here."

"But I heard it." Relief and confusion scrunched her face. She held her belly with one hand and pushed her body down, against Kevin's.

"Heard what?" Kevin said, putting an arm around her.

"The water."

"A dream. Go to sleep."

And after an hour or more of lying there, listening, straining to hear what she did or didn't before, Kevin's arm heavy on her chest, a bag of sand holding her still, sleep washed back over her.

§

A week later, Jen woke again. The same sounds. The same panic. She sat up and pinched herself, looked at the clock, looked at Kevin, sleeping. She was definitely awake. She held her breath, listened. Yes. She heard it and she knew, pictured it.

Water pouring into more water, swirling around the basement staircase, dumping into low corners, paint cans bobbing and bumping into one another.

She reached for Kevin. She wasn't wrong, she wasn't dreaming.

"Kevin," she said, squeezing his bare shoulder, leaning over him in the dark. "Kevin, I can hear it and it's real, can't you hear it? Kevin, listen!"

"Jen!" he mumbled. "Enough. There's no fucking water."

He didn't move. She shook him.

"Jen, I said stop! Dammit!" He reached behind him and shoved her—surely harder than he meant to, surely he wasn't really awake, at least not all the way.

Her body had been curled up, weight balanced on her tailbone, and she toppled off the side of the bed, one hand flailing, the other on her stomach. She caught her temple on the corner of the nightstand, landed on her knees, gasping, head ringing. She touched her face. No blood.

Slowly, she stood. Kevin was either asleep or pretending. She could still hear the water. If he wasn't going to deal with it, she would. She put on her robe and made her way downstairs, around the corner and through the living room, into the kitchen, down the steps, the planks rough on her bare feet. Her head ached and dread pooled in her gut.

She flicked the light switch at the little landing where the stairway turned ninety degrees. The last four steps were under water. It lapped against the fieldstone walls and as she stared, it rose higher, pouring in from an unseen source, creeping toward her, touching her toes, so cold, and she knew she should back up, climb the steps, get out, but she couldn't make her body listen, was something moving in the water?

And then it reached the hem of her robe, dark shapes, below the surface, and then she felt it on her shins, and that's when she remembered to close her eyes and scream.

Moments later, but it felt like forever, Kevin's hands were on her arms and he was shaking her, holding her up, saying her name, how many times? She opened her eyes to his angry face, no—worried, and looked down, ready to warn him, but it was all gone.

The steps were dry. Nothing moved in the basement but her heaving chest. She sputtered, then she cried, and before long, she was back in bed, Kevin rubbing her back and talking about pregnancy hormones and bad dreams and how falling out of bed probably didn't help and needing to go to the doctor for a checkup anyway and shh baby shh it would be better in the morning.

§

A few days later, Jen sat in a chilly exam room in a thin paper gown, waiting for the ultrasound technician. She'd told the doctor, called in special for her, about the sounds of water in the night, what Kevin said, how she'd heard it again, a third night and a fourth, and from the way the doctor answered she knew he'd said the same things to women before—pregnancy, hormones, changes, nightmares, sleepwalking, how it was all natural.

"Your body is doing amazing things right now, growing another human, and you have to be patient with miracles," he said, making notes, looking up to smile, looking back down at her file, pen scratching, scratching.

"With these fluctuations, emotions run high, and of course those carry over to the sleeping hours. Try to relax. Ah, here's Letisha."

A young woman walked into the room, sneakers squeaking on the clean floor. Her scrubs were fluorescent pink, her hair done up in tiny braids. "Ready?" she asked Jen. More smiles all around. The doctor left.

The gel on her belly was too cold, the fluorescent lights too bright, but then Jen heard the whooshing of her baby's feisty heartbeat, saw the white outline of a little body on the monitor, heard Letisha laugh and say, "Here we go! It's your baby!"

Kevin was at work. He couldn't get the day off. Jen had said it was fine; she knew the technician would give her pictures to show him later. But at that moment, she wished it were Kevin, not a stranger, holding her hand.

Jen couldn't tear her eyes from the screen. A head. A torso. An arm.

"That looks like a tail," she said, letting go of Letisha's hand to point.

Letisha laughed. "They all sort of look like tadpoles when they're inside, curled up like that. Cute little pollywogs. But trust me, this one's right on track. I'm just going to take some measurements."

Jen stared. The baby twisted to the left, back to the right. Stretched an arm.

"Do you want to know the sex?" Letisha asked.

Jen nodded and learned she would have a little boy. Just what Kevin wanted.

§

Despite the sealant and two layers of dove gray satin finish paint, Jen still caught whiffs of mildew in the living room. But Kevin said there was no smell, so when they watched movies together on their lumpy old couch Jen breathed through her mouth and whenever Kevin noticed she'd say, smiling, that her allergies were acting up.

§

For Valentine's Day, Jen surprised her husband with a fancy dinner, cooked on their new stove that he had brought home from a scratch-n-dent tent sale. Strip steaks, baked potatoes with butter and cheese, steamed broccoli, and ice cream for dessert.

Jen ate as much as Kevin and then offered to wash the dishes.

"That was delicious, babe," he said, and kissed her, his lips cold from the ice cream.

He opened another beer and went up to the room he already called his office. A minute later, Jen heard the sounds of a video game seep through the ceiling above her.

She hummed while she filled the sink and plugged the drain, not bothering to wait for the water to get hot. It was no tune in particular, just sounds she made because she was happy and full and felt so lucky. She looked through the window above the double sink at the darkening back yard, the snow-covered grass, a few scrubby bushes and then the bank of the creek where the yard fell away.

She contemplated baby names as her hands reached to find plates and bowls and spoons, swirling a dishrag over them and moving them to the other basin.

Jacob, she thought. *Samuel. David.* Her father's name was Patrick, and she liked that. Kevin voted for Kevin Junior.

They had a few months still to decide, but Jen wanted to refer to the baby inside her by name. When she spoke to him, usually when Kevin wasn't home, she tried asking what he liked, saying kick once for yes, twice for no. But he only kicked when he wanted to.

A sharp pain in her finger made her jump. *Shit.* She should have washed the steak knives separate. She pulled her hands out of the sudsy water, expecting blood, reaching already for the dishtowel on the counter, but it wasn't a cut.

Hanging onto her ring finger was a crayfish the size of a cigarette lighter, pinching hard with the bigger of his two claws. Jen made a sound more like a squeak than a scream. Then she laughed.

But it hurt, so she ran the water until it was colder and doused the crayfish until he let go. She caught him with her other palm stretched flat, so he couldn't get another grip on her.

She knew the pipes in the house were bad, rusty, but this was the first crayfish she'd found in the sink. She thought about yelling for Kevin, but decided to let him relax.

He'd been putting in long hours lately, picking up overtime, paying for stuff around the house. She grabbed a thick cardigan from the back of the couch and draped it over her shoulders, careful not to knock the crayfish off her palm.

Then she traded her slippers for Kevin's work boots and slipped out the back door.

Her feet punched through the top crust of ice on the snow. It was a short walk to the water's edge. Ice crept along the banks, but at its center the creek still flowed fast, tumbling over small rocks and smooth sections of shale.

Jen knew the crayfish would be fine; she'd set him in the shallows and he'd burrow into the mud, his mottled brown body disappearing. But she felt reluctant to put him down.

She held him closer to her face, squinting in the dark, trying to find his eyes.

"Do you have a name?" she whispered. "What about David? Patrick? Kevin Junior?" She laughed.

The crayfish didn't answer. Didn't kick or pinch. His eyes moved, seemed to focus on her face, then held still.

§

"Jen!" she heard, and felt a rough pull on her arm, knocking her off balance. She fell onto one knee in the creek, looked down with a shock at the frigid water rippling around Kevin's boots on her feet, filling them, numbing her toes. The crayfish was gone.

"What the fuck, Jen!" Kevin shouted. "What are you doing? I've been calling you for twenty minutes. Why are you out here? It's freezing! Are those my goddamned work boots? Jen, I need those!"

Jen shook herself, stood up and stepped out of the creek. "I'm sorry," she said. "I lost track of time. There was a crayfish, and I—"

"Get inside," Kevin cut her off. "You shouldn't be out here."

He held onto her hand and pulled her behind him. Jen stumbled in the snow but Kevin didn't slow down. She couldn't feel the soles of her feet. When they got inside, he stomped back upstairs, muttering about his boots.

Jen changed her clothes, put on socks and slippers and her robe, and plugged in her hair dryer to see what she could do about the boots.

§

That night, she heard the water again, and she told herself she was dreaming, and she felt her finger throb, and she told herself that was maybe a dream too, and she thought of or dreamed of crayfish eyes, and of tadpoles swimming, and the cold creek rushing around her, and she thought of or dreamed of reaching out for help and finding only more water.

§

After four days of steady rain, the flood warning sounded. It came as a beeping on Jen's cell phone, emergency notification, neon letters flashing on the screen. It was just past four p.m.

In April, everyone expected rain. They expected melting. They expected warming temperatures, the sun showing itself after too many bleak months. But it happened all at once; more rain than they wanted, more melting than they thought, temperatures too warm to be welcome.

Jen was putting baby clothes away in the little white dresser—0-3 months in one drawer, burp cloths in another, larger clothing in the last. When the warning showed on her phone, she yelled for Kevin.

"The creek is already swelling, almost beyond the banks," she told him, holding up her phone, glancing out the window toward the creek. "This is saying the temps we're getting are too warm. There'll be ice jams. It'll all wash down from the hills and we'll get flooding. Do you think we'll be okay?"

"There's flooding all around here in the spring," Kevin said, leaning over to kiss her cheek. "We might get a little water in the basement, but I'll move everything up off the floor. Plus, we have flood insurance. We'll be fine. Stop worrying."

Jen smiled and returned to her task. Kevin went into his office. She listened to the rain. It seemed to be coming down harder; faster than steady, faster than safe. She put a stack of green and blue onesies away. Her phone beeped again.

EVACUATION RECOMMENDED FOR AREAS IN CATTARAUGUS COUNTY. Their county. She clicked a link, which took her to a map. Their area. Their house, their creek. She yelled for Kevin again, flicking her eyes from the rain outside to her phone screen.

"What, Jen?" he said, strong arms spanning the doorframe, looking at her with a mix of fatigue and thinning patience.

She showed him her phone. She explained. The warnings. The map. The flood zone.

"Jen," he said, and she thought he was using her name too much. She took a step back. "We knew the house was by a creek. We knew we'd have to get a little extra insurance. We did that. This is YOUR dream house. You had to have it. You HAD to buy it." His voice was getting louder. Little red spots showed on his cheeks. He took a step forward.

Jen tried to stay calm. "No, I know, I know, honey," she said. "And I love our house so much, and our baby is going to love our house, and I just wonder if we should pack some stuff and maybe go to your parents' for a couple of days, just until this storm settles down, and—"

Then he was in front of her, too close, spit flecking the corners of his mouth as he said they weren't running away because of a little rain, a little fucking water, and it was Jen who had to have this place, who had to tie up every goddamn dollar in it so she could live some bullshit fairy tale while he worked his ass off and didn't she see how patient he was being, how she was testing his limits, how hard he was trying to be a good husband? Didn't she?

Jen tried to backpedal, fear making her voice shrill, manic. "Yeah, of course. Maybe the storm won't be so bad. Maybe this warning—" she held up her phone again, "maybe it's just like a precaution. Just, like if people want to be prepared—"

Kevin slapped his hand against the side of the crib. Jen jumped.

"Are you saying I'm NOT prepared, Jen?" he asked. He wasn't blinking. "I fucking TOLD you that I'd move things in the basement. I fucking TOLD you we would be fine. It's like you don't trust me to take care of my family!"

Jen shook her head side to side, too fast.

"I think it's time we give THIS a break, don't you?" he asked, and dove for her phone, pulling it from her hand.

"No!" Jen said, reaching for it, terror making her brave, trying to take it back. She couldn't be in this storm with no phone. She was eight months pregnant. She couldn't be cut off. Panic rose in her like steam with no vent. Her fingers grasped the edge of the phone, and Kevin flung his arm wide, backhanding Jen across the cheek, sending her body spinning, crumpling into the dresser behind her, one drawer still pulled out, cutting into her chest above her left breast. For a moment, she couldn't breathe, shock making the room, Kevin, the storm, her pain, stand still.

Kevin loomed over her, arm extended.

"The baby!" Jen cried, alternating sobs with gasps. "Don't!" She grabbed a teddy bear that had fallen near her, held up its plush body like a shield, like it was enough to protect her from her husband's quick temper.

He snatched it from her, throwing it into the crib. He picked her up by her left elbow, hauling her to her feet. He held the phone in front of her face, shaking her with every word. "You. Can't. Have. This," he said. "You need to calm down."

He turned to leave, tried to shut the door behind him, close her in, but Jen rushed after him, chasing him into the hallway as thunder shook the sky outside and rumbled through the house.

She caught up with him at the top of the stairs, grasping the hem of his t-shirt, ready to beg. Before he turned on her, she saw past him, saw that downstairs, under the front door, water puddled, seeping farther into their home, spreading across the worn wooden floorboards. She tried to point to it, to tell Kevin, but his eyes were on her face, lips curled in a sneer.

He shoved her, letting go of the banister to do it. She fell back, away from him, away from the yawning staircase, losing her hold on his shirt and slamming her spine against the doorframe opposite. But he fell too, his anger backfiring, sending his body sailing out over the stairs, over nothing but a drop to the unforgiving wood below, his yell blending with Jen's scream before he hit, the crunch of bone breaking, landing at the bottom, slapping into the frigid water that was still coming, coming, that was rising.

Jen yelled her husband's name, tried to stand, to go after him, to help, but pain held her down. A shuddering cramp buckled her body, left her retching on hands and knees, throwing her back into spasms.

Kevin yelled, but she couldn't make out what he said. *The baby*, she thought. Then, *my phone*. But it was gone, somewhere down below with Kevin, in the water.

Jen crawled, every movement an effort, back into the baby's room. She heard the sound of glass breaking downstairs. The windows. A rush of more water, a crash she couldn't identify. Kevin's voice, another crash.

She slammed the door behind her, trying to shut out the danger and the ruin, reached to pull an afghan down from the side of the crib. She felt a pressure between her legs, then a release. Her leggings were soaked, the smell of creek water—but that couldn't be—sharp in her nose, filling the room.

She gagged and then pulled off her leggings, heaved her body around, her head against the crib. Contractions rocked her frame, pelvis to shoulders. She sobbed to no one about how it was too soon. She called out to Kevin, over and over, but couldn't hear him anymore.

There was only the sound of water, of her own terrified voice, of a woman roaring alone in a storm.

§

It got much worse before it got any better. Her body was torn in half. Her insides emptied. Blood and other fluids swirled together on the floor. And after the rain quieted, when Jen was too tired to do anything except breathe, but before the sound of an approaching boat motor signaled their rescue, she heard, for the first time, her baby's feeble cries.

§

A hundred-year flood, they were calling it. Kevin's body had been washed clear of the house, located two days later. A blessing she hadn't been the one to find him, said the officer who visited Jen at the hospital.

"The way he looked—what the water did to him," she said. "You wouldn't want to see him. It's better this way."

Jen nodded, nursed her baby. Nodded again.

§

Between life insurance and the other policies, the damage had been undone by June. The windows unbroken. The house unflooded. Even the damp smell gone.

§

July, late afternoon. Jen waded into the creek, carrying Patrick, walking until she stepped down into a deeper pool beneath a low waterfall. She sat on a natural shale shelf and settled him in her lap.

His algae-green eyes lit up when he felt tiny ripples brush his naked belly. She held him in front of her and the water held them both, the gentle current flowing around their bodies. Patrick kicked his chubby legs and bobbed his arms up and down, splashing her.

He was a natural.

Jen watched her son, listened to his burbling laugh and to the running creekwater and to a flickering dragonfly off to her left and then she hummed along, no tune in particular.

READERS' DISCUSSION GUIDE

One of the themes in SIX O'CLOCK HOUSE & OTHER STRANGE TALES is redemption. Which of these characters most deserves the forgiveness or reprieve they seek, and why?

In several of these stories, nature will ultimately have its revenge. Are those endings happy or sad? In what ways?

Some of these characters sacrifice themselves for loved ones. Would you do the same if you were in their situations? Why or why not?

Sometimes there is no hero coming to the rescue—the victims or would-be victims must save themselves. Which of these self-saviors did you cheer the loudest for? What about them made you feel that way?

Which character was the most fun to hate in the collection? Why do they deserve to have the most rotten vegetables thrown at them?

Readers get a few stories of "love gone wrong" here. If these characters were your friends, how would you convince them to "dump the chump" (or chumpette) and run?

Not every character in the collection lives to fight another day. If you could spare or resurrect one of them, which would it be, and why would they be worthy of the second chance?

Last question: Which of these ghosts is your favorite? Why?

ABOUT THE AUTHOR

Rebecca Cuthbert is a dark fiction and poetry writer living in Western New York. She loves ghost stories, folklore, witchy women, and anything that involves nature getting revenge. For publications and information, visit rebeccacuthbert.com.

ADDITIONAL TITLES BY REBECCA CUTHBERT

IN MEMORY OF EXOSKELETONS, poetry collection, Alien Buddha Press, 2023, winner of the 2024 Imadjinn Award for Best Poetry Collection

CREEP THIS WAY: HOW TO BECOME A HORROR WRITER WITH 24 TIPS TO GET YOU GHOULING, how-to and memoir, Seamus & Nunzio Productions, 2024, nominated for a 2024 Golden Scoop Award

SELF-MADE MONSTERS, hybrid collection of feminist horror, Alien Budda Press, 2024

DOWN IN THE DARK DEEP WHERE THE PUDDLERS DWELL, children's horror picture book, Malediction and AEA Press, 2024

ACKNOWLEDGMENTS

There are many, many people to thank for their help and guidance in the creation of *Six O'Clock House & Other Strange Tales*, especially since one of these stories was first drafted in 2007.

First, and always first, thank you to my husband Joel. I have had him in my life longer than any of these stories, and it's largely through his encouragement and support that I am a writer at all. He makes space, in ways both practical and emotional, for me to do this–write weird, dark stories; go to events and conventions; spend hours online or in my head. Plus he's handsome and funny, and the only person I always want to hang out with. Thank you forever. I love you.

Next, to the folks who worked with me on some of these stories' earliest drafts: Mark Brazaitis, Janet Peery, Heather Frese, Kelly Sundberg; later, Sarah Reichert, Sara Lucas, Keema Waterfield. They met my oddities and didn't flinch. Thanks, guys. I'm so lucky to know you.

To friends who helped me polish later drafts, who beta read, who traded feedback with me, who offered encouragement and kept me at my desk: Jonathan Gensler, Eliza Broadbent, Christopher O'Halloran, James Sabata, Sarah Gerkensmeyer. Thank you so much.

To my writing mentors and the groups of writers they nurture: Moaner Lawrence and Fright Club, Lindsay Merbaum and the Study Coven. Thank you all. I grew so much with you, and will continue to do so.

A special thank you to Lindsay Merbaum, who was so generous in writing the introduction to this collection. Thanks, you beautiful witch.

To all the talented writers who lent me their voices in blurbs for the book: Sarah Gerkensmeyer and Chris O'Halloran (again!), Jamie Flanagan, Lyndsey Croal, TJ Price. Thank you for your kindness.

To all the real-life people and places who inspired these stories: Thank you for the source material. (And yes–Butch is pretty much just my dad.)

To the editors and publishers who put some of these stories in print well before they ever united to become a collection: thank you for helping me find my feet in the world of publishing.

And finally, to the team at Watertower Hill Publishing, who gave these stories a forever home. They weren't afraid of a literary-genre hybrid; they looked beyond labels and saw me and my characters for who we are: monstrous little cryptids and chimeras, not wholly irredeemable.

To my publisher (and formatter and marketing guru), Joshua Loyd Fox; my talented editor and soul sister in all things beautiful and creepy, Heather Daughrity; and Susan Roddey, the cover artist who brings Josh's visions to life: thank you. It means so much that you welcomed me into the WTHP family.